THE SORCERER'S APPRENTICE

Raven Hill Mysteries

THE SORCERER'S APPRENTICE

Raven Hill Mysteries 2

Emily Rodda
&
John St Claire

Hodder
Children's
Books

a division of Hodder Headline plc

Series concept copyright © Emily Rodda 1994
Text copyright © Ashton Scholastic 1994

First published in Australia in 1994 by
Ashton Scholastic Pty Limited

First published in Great Britain in 1995
by Hodder Children's Books

10 9 8 7 6 5 4 3 2 1

A Catalogue record for this book is available from the British
Library

ISBN 0 340 62993 2

Typeset by Avon Dataset Ltd, Bidford-on-Avon
Printed and bound in Great Britain by
Cox & Wyman Ltd, Reading, Berks.

Hodder Children's Books
a division of Hodder Headline plc
338 Euston Road
London NW1 3BH

Contents

1

The Gripper

The name Jack the Gripper started as a joke, but there was nothing funny about what the thief himself got up to. He was vicious, always attacking from behind, whipping his arm around his victims' necks and pulling it so tight they couldn't breathe. There was also the hard point of a gun barrel in the back.

Then he'd grab their bag or wallet and whisper, 'Now I'm going to let you up and you're going to shut up. Got it? Keep your eyes closed till you count to fifty! One look at me and I'll be the last thing you ever see.'

It was always the same method and the same words. By the time a victim finished counting, the Gripper was gone. And the strange thing was, nobody ever saw a man running from the scene of the crime. Nobody ever saw anything suspicious at all. It was like the Gripper disappeared into thin air.

He usually went for his victims after dark, but occasionally an old man or woman alone in a car park in broad daylight would be too much of a temptation for him. So he'd rip them off as quick as a flash—and still get clean away.

I heard this lady on a talk-back radio show saying that she thought he had supernatural powers. That's what she reckoned, anyway. Of course I don't believe in things like that. But even with cops crawling all over Raven Hill the attacks continued and nobody ever saw a thing. The Gripper was smart, no doubt about that.

At first there were robberies once or twice a week, but soon they were happening almost every day. The Gripper hadn't killed anyone yet, but the police were obviously worried that he might. The attacks were getting more violent. More and more victims ended up on the ground, gasping for breath and had to be taken to hospital for observation.

Of course there were a lot of sick jokes going around at Raven Hill High. But we weren't kidding ourselves. Everybody was walking around town looking over their shoulders for Jack the Gripper—even us kids.

Anyway, let me tell you how Teen Power Inc. got involved in all this ...

It was Friday afternoon and I was sitting in English about to die of boredom. Mr Larson was going on and on in this really quiet voice like he was trying to hypnotise us or something. He's a nice guy, Mr Larson, but his classes aren't what you'd call exciting.

You are getting sleepy, very sleepy, Tom, I was thinking.

No matter how hard I concentrated my mind kept wandering. He might just as well have been talking to us in Mongolian.

When was that final bell going to ring?!

Richelle was sitting in front of me and a little to the side, studying her fingernails. Good old glam-puss Richelle. She wasn't listening to a word of what old Larson was saying either, but she had this look on her face like she was really interested. She kept nodding her head as if she was agreeing with him.

Anyway, I opened my sketch book and started drawing her. She looked kind of like Snow White or something. Her hair was all in one neat piece, like it was plastic or it was held together with a kilo of hair spray. She must have spent three hours working on it before school to get it like that.

Richelle *always* looked great. She was one of those people who could get lost in a rainforest for a week and come out looking like a cover girl. And I'm the kind of guy who'd look daggy wearing a tuxedo. Not that I've ever worn a tuxedo.

She turned her head, saw what I was doing and gave me the dirtiest look. Sort of a how-dare-you-draw-a-picture-of-me-without-my-permission look. 'Stop that!' she mouthed silently at me.

When was that bell going to ring? Maybe the clock was stopped?

Of the six of us in Teen Power—me, Elmo, Liz, Sunny, Nick, and Richelle—Richelle is the one with the charmed life. Teachers eat out of her hand. She can do anything and not get busted.

Richelle: 'I couldn't finish my homework because I broke a fingernail when I went to the airport to see my grandmother off to Paris.'

3

Teacher: 'That's okay, Richelle. Just hand it in when you can.'

All right, that's a bit of an exaggeration—but only a bit.

I'm just the opposite. I'm always in deep strife.

Me: 'I'm sorry I didn't finish my homework but my whole family was wiped out when a crop-dusting plane hit our house. What with four funerals in one day there wasn't enough time to finish my assignment, but I'll hand it in tomorrow.'

Teacher: 'Too bad, Tom, but you should have allowed time for emergencies. I'm going to have to give you an F.'

You just get a feeling that if a hundred-dollar note fell from the sky it would land in Richelle's pocket. Or some guy would pick it up off the ground and say, 'Excuse me, Miss, but I think you dropped something.'

Me, I'd probably get arrested for theft.

Cop: 'I don't know who you stole it from, son, but you must have stolen it from somebody. Come with us to the police station. With any luck you'll be out of prison in forty years with good behaviour.'

Anyway, there I was sketching Richelle and trying to listen to Mr Larson when the kid behind me dropped a note over my shoulder and into my lap.

Carefully, I unfolded the paper and read it. It said:

> New gig. Meet corner of Wattle & Burke streets
> <u>straight</u> after school. Don't go to the Glen.
> Don't go home. Be there or beware!

The note was from Nick. It wasn't signed but it was his handwriting. And who else would call a *job* a *gig*? I turned around and there he was at the back of the class ignoring me and pretending to listen to Mr Larson. Typical Nick.

Another Teen Power job, I thought. Good. I sure could use the money. I gave Nick the thumbs up and he just rolled his eyes like I shouldn't even be looking at him. He was as bad as Richelle.

'Tom Moysten!' Mr Larson yelled. 'You're not paying attention!'

I whipped around in my chair and closed my sketch book.

'Yes I am,' I said.

(Laughter.)

'Then tell me what I just said.'

You know how sometimes you can repeat what someone just said even if you didn't really hear it at the time? Well I couldn't. Not this time, anyway.

'You said I wasn't paying attention,' I said.

(More laughter.)

Mr Larson wasn't amused.

'Oh, a comedian,' he said. 'Perhaps you'd like to stand up here and tell a few jokes.'

'No thanks.'

'Afraid to make a fool of yourself?' he asked.

'No, that's your job,' I said.

(Long, loud laughter.)

I really didn't mean to say it. It kind of just slipped out. Mr Larson folded his arms and stared at me. I could feel myself blushing, which made everything worse.

Just then the bell rang. Everybody started packing up.

'Tom,' Mr Larson ordered. 'Stay right where you are.'

But I wasn't in strife this time, not really. Mr Larson just said he was going to let me off but that I had to pay attention from now on.

'Yes, sir.'

Mr Larson isn't a bad bloke. He and Brian—that's my stepfather—are good mates. Brian teaches ancient history at Raven Hill High. You always see him and Mr Larson together in the staffroom.

'And Tom?'

'Yes?'

'You've got a good sense of humour.'

'Thanks.'

'But try not to use it all the time,' he said. 'Give it a rest.'

'Yes, sir.'

2

Teen Power together

I ran to catch up with Nick and Richelle. They were chatting, heads together. Two of a kind.

When I got close I realised that they were talking so much that they didn't realise I was behind them. I couldn't help myself: I got really close and then put an arm around Richelle's neck.

'Close your eyes and count to fifty!' I whispered.

Of course I didn't do it really hard and Richelle just turned around and gave me a shove.

'Cut it out!' she yelled. 'That's not funny!'

'Grow up, Moysten!' said Nick. 'And what are you doing here anyhow? What's the story? Didn't Larson keep you in?'

'Only because he wanted my advice.'

'Be serious!'

'Would I lie to you? He wants to know how to make his classes more entertaining,' I said. 'He asked me to help him develop his sense of humour. We start next week. It could take a while.'

'You know what, Tom?' Richelle said. She was still

rubbing her throat like I'd really hurt her—which I definitely hadn't. 'You're a real dag.'

'I do my best,' I said.

'And give me that!'

Richelle grabbed at the sketchbook but I put it behind my back. I knew she wouldn't try to fight me for it. That wasn't her style. Besides, it might mess up her hair.

'I just want to see the drawing you did of me,' she said.

'It's not finished,' I said.

'So what?'

'So you won't like it.'

Nick looked over like he was bored or something.

'Just show it to her, Moysten,' he said.

'No way,' I said.

Liz, Sunny and Elmo were waiting at the corner up ahead. Here we all were: the whole Teen Power gang together in the same spot at the same time. Considering it was Friday afternoon, this was pretty amazing. We were with them in a minute.

Liz was the first to speak.

'Thanks for coming,' she said. 'Sorry I couldn't give you any more warning. I got a phone call last night from Sidney Foy, the guy who owns Sid's Magic Shop across the street there.'

I looked across at the block of old shops, most of them boarded up. The paint on Sid's sign was peeling so badly that you couldn't read all the letters. If you looked at it quickly, you'd think it said: ID'S MAG   HOP.

'Oh, that place,' Nick said.

'He wants some help cleaning,' Liz explained. 'That's all

he said. I don't know how much or what kind.'

'Cleaning?' Nick said. 'Well that counts me out.'

'What do you mean?'

'What do you mean, "What do I mean?" Look at me. Do I look like a cleaning lady?'

'Hey! That's sexist!' Sunny objected.

'All right, a cleaning *person*, okay?'

'Well if that's the way you feel, Nick, you shouldn't be in Teen Power,' Liz snapped. 'Everybody does everything, okay? That's the deal. No picking and choosing. Otherwise it's unfair. And bad for business, too.'

Of course Liz was right. I didn't mind the Teen Power work, but Nick and Richelle only wanted to work when it was easy or fun. They probably got more allowance than the rest of us put together. Of course they spent it as fast as they got it. Richelle had more new clothes than she knew what to do with. So did Nick, for that matter.

'I'm just no good at cleaning,' Nick pleaded.

'Yeah, sure,' said Sunny. 'Like we are, right? Like we were all born with cleaners' chromosomes and you weren't, right?'

I liked the way Sunny didn't let him get away with anything.

'Are you in or out, Nick?' Liz asked. 'Remember, if you're out, you're out for good.'

Nick waited for a minute before answering and then said, 'Oh, okay, I'm in. But I'm allergic to dust.'

Everyone laughed.

'Come off it, Nick,' Sunny said. 'You're allergic to work, that's what you're allergic to.'

'Sunny, that's not nice,' Nick said.

I *am* allergic to dust—and grasses and cats and dogs and you name it. But I didn't say anything. Partly because I didn't want to sound like I was making excuses, but mainly because I *loved* the idea of working in Sid's Magic Shop. It was such a great place. I only lived a few streets away, and I'd been in it lots of times though I can't say I spent a lot of money. It was just a good place to go to look around at everything.

'Right,' Liz said. 'Now let's go over and talk to Mr Foy. We listen and then we talk about it between ourselves afterwards, okay?'

'OK, boss,' Nick said meekly.

She gave him a crushing look and stalked off across the road.

There was definitely something strange about Sid Foy, or Sigmund the Sorcerer, as he was also known. That had been his stage name when he had a magic show that toured all over the country. He reckoned that he'd performed in every town and city with a population of over two hundred. I didn't think that was possible but I never knew what to believe when Sid was talking.

Anyway, he did all those old tricks like sawing someone in half and pulling pigeons out of his sleeves. And he was also a terrific ventriloquist. He had a dummy, Jacko, that he sat up on the counter and sometimes when you asked him a question, the dummy answered.

So why did he stop doing his magic show and open a magic shop? Simple. He was in a car accident. He hit a kangaroo late at night and the car went into a ditch and flipped over. He almost died from the injuries. When he got out of hospital six months later, he was missing his right arm and his right eye.

He had an artificial arm with a sort of hook on the end instead of a hand, but he didn't always wear it. He also had an artificial eye, made of glass. It looked quite real, but I don't think he was comfortable with it, because a lot of the time he just wore a patch over his blind eye instead.

Now if all that happened to me I reckon I'd just sit around and watch TV for the rest of my life and feel sorry for myself. Not Sid. Every time I'd been in the shop he was laughing and joking like everything was okay. Well, maybe it was.

Anyway, that was Sigmund the Sorcerer.

3

The magic gig

You know how when you go into some shops there's a ping or a bell or a buzzer or something to say that a customer just came in? Well Sid had one of those except it wasn't a ping or a bell or a buzzer—it was a shriek like in a horror movie followed by a mad, evil laugh. It was really great. Richelle went in first, and she wasn't ready for it. She jumped right back out the door, screaming.

Admittedly, Sid had the sound turned up too high and it really did give you a shock even if you knew about it.

'It's just a doorbell,' I said, rubbing my foot where she'd trodden on it. 'It won't bite you.'

She shook back her hair and made a face. 'How *stupid*,' she said.

We all trooped in and looked around the dark and dusty room. A single light, dangling from a frayed cord, lit the middle of the shop. There was a counter over on one side.

'This place needs more than cleaning,' Nick said. 'It needs knocking down and rebuilding.'

'Shhh!' ordered Liz.

There was no-one else in the shop: no customers, no sign

of Sid. The place looked like something out of a science-fiction movie, all those horrible rubber masks on the wall and then shelves and shelves of things in boxes, collecting dust.

I started looking around at all the jokes and tricks: itching powder, rubber fingers, plastic ice cubes with spiders in them, drinking glasses with holes in them so everything dribbles down your shirt.

I picked up a huge rubber spider and held it out to Richelle.

'Tom! If you do, I'll kill you!' she screamed. 'You put that thing down. Put it down!'

'I'm just showing it to you.'

'Yeah, sure,' she said.

'Mr Foy! We're here!' Liz called out. 'Teen Power!'

No answer.

'He's probably gone out of business and gone bush,' Nick muttered. 'Nobody ever comes in here. It's got to be the stupidest business in town. Kids don't want this old stuff. It's like something out of the dark ages. This isn't a shop, it's a museum.'

'Nick!' Liz whispered. 'He might hear you.'

'So what if he does?'

'I like this place,' I admitted.

'Do you ever come in here?' Nick asked.

'Sure.'

'What's the last thing you bought in here?' he asked.

'I can't remember.'

Nick gave me one of his smug looks. He was right, I hardly bought anything. But there was something about the place I liked.

'See? Museum,' Nick said. 'Everybody comes to look but nobody buys. Either this guy is rich and doesn't care how he makes a living or he's living on fresh air.'

The others were looking around the shelves. Sunny picked up three rubber balls and started juggling them.

Richelle picked up a plastic cow. It mooed and stuck out its tongue.

'Oh, yuck!' she said. 'That's *off*!'

'Let me tell you something, Tom,' Nick said. 'Any business that has to depend on kids' allowances is a stupid business. How much money can you squeeze out of a kid? They're always poor. It's parents that have dough. If I had a shop I'd sell something that rich people buy like Armani suits, Cartier watches, Gucci shoes, stuff like that—things that cost.'

'Who's got money for those things in Raven Hill?' I asked.

'There are a few people,' Nick said. 'Anyway, who said anything about Raven Hill? I'd open a shop where the big money is. Look at this place, it's a hole. Kids come in here and play around with things but they don't have any money. They probably break more than they buy.'

Having got rid of the rude cow, Richelle was on the far side of the shop looking at the things on the counter. Propped up against the cash register was Jacko, Sid's ventriloquist doll. He had red freckles, a looney wise-guy sort of expression and brown hair that stuck out all over the place.

'Look!' she laughed. 'It's a Tom doll!'

'Very funny,' I said.

As Richelle reached up to touch Jacko's face, his eyes snapped open.

14

'She touched me! She touched me!' Jacko yelled, his head swivelling from side to side. 'I'll sue! Call the police!'

Richelle let out a blood-curdling scream and fell back against a small table, knocking plastic snakes and cockroaches all over the place.

'That does it!' she yelled. 'I'm getting out of here!'

'What a good idea,' the dummy said. 'Mind if I come too?'

With that, Sid raised his head above the counter. He had on his black eye-patch and his shirt-sleeve pinned to his shoulder.

Liz stared at him in disbelief.

'So this is Teen Power Inc.,' he said. 'My, my, only six of you? I reckon this job could take the whole army.'

'And the navy,' Jacko said.

'Thank you, Jacko,' said Sid. 'But, seriously, there's only enough room back there for one or two people. Which one of you is Elizabeth Free?'

'I am,' said Liz. 'What sort of cleaning do you want us to do?'

'Didn't I explain that on the phone? No, I guess I didn't. Very forgetful, I'm afraid. Better follow me,' he said, walking towards a door at the back of the shop with his hand still in Jacko's back. 'There's a storeroom here at the back that needs a good clean out. I'm afraid it's full of . . . well . . . what can I call it?'

'Junk,' Jacko said.

'Thank you, Jacko.'

'You're welcome, Sid.'

'But it's not *all* junk. There are some valuable treasures in

15

there so I don't just want to throw everything into the back lane. So I guess you'd call this a sorting and sifting job. I'll be here to give advice but I can't lend a hand.'

'You've only got one hand, Sid,' Jacko said.

'You don't say, Jacko.'

'I do say, Sid.'

'But I can keep an eye on things.'

'You've only got one of those, too, Sid,' the dummy said.

'That'll be enough of that, Jacko,' Sid said.

Richelle just rolled her eyes at the corny humour.

'This place has got to be a bit of a fire trap,' Sid said. 'When I lived in the flat upstairs I didn't care. So if the place went up, the place went up. There were just me and Jacko here and we're disposable.'

'Speak for yourself, Sid,' Jacko said.

'But now I've moved out to the caravan park and rented the flat to a nice young couple. We can't have anything happening to them.'

The storeroom was stacked from floor to ceiling with piles of boxes and magazines and old clothes. There was just a narrow aisle down the middle leading to the back door.

'You can see the problem,' Sid said. 'It's so cramped in here that I think only one or two of you can fit. I reckon there's at least a week's work for one person if he or she spends, say, two hours on it after school.'

'At least,' Nick muttered, looking around.

'So what'll it be?' Sid asked. 'One person or two? And when can you start?'

Through the dusty window at the back I could see Sid's tenants go up the outside stairs to the flat above. They looked like they were in their early twenties. He had his arm around her, helping her. She was obviously expecting a baby—*very* obviously.

Liz went into the storeroom, studying it for a minute. A mouse ran along the aisle and then disappeared. Richelle, standing beside me now, shuddered.

'Oh, yuck,' she muttered.

'We'll have to discuss it, Mr Foy,' Liz said, coming back.

'Just don't leave me up in the air too long,' said Sid. 'I want to get this fixed up as soon as possible.'

'Don't worry,' Liz reassured him. 'We won't leave you up in the air. I'll get back to you tonight.'

'Up in the air?' Jacko exploded. 'Get back to us? That's not a girl—that's a boomerang.'

'Now be polite, Jacko,' Sid said.

'Sorry, Sid,' said Jacko.

Later, out on the footpath, Nick turned to me. 'Well? Did you figure out how he does it?'

'Does what?' I asked.

'Stays in business. It's the upstairs flat. He moved out to the caravan park because it's cheap. He rents the flat for more than he's paying and that's how he keeps the shop open.'

'You're just guessing,' I said.

'I'll bet I'm right,' Nick answered.

4

A meeting
at the *Pen*

Usually we hold our meetings in a place called the Glen, a patch of bush beside Raven Hill park. But this day Elmo had to get back to help his father at the *Pen* office. The *Pen* was his dad's newspaper. Since one of Teen Power's jobs was to deliver it around Raven Hill every Thursday before school, Mr Zimmer (we called him Zim) didn't mind us meeting there. In fact, Teen Power Inc. had once helped keep the *Pen* from going out of business, so everyone in the office was always nice to us.

'Come on, let's work this out quickly,' Liz said when we were all together. 'I've got to get out of here soon to do Miss Plummer's shopping.'

'And I'm just really tired out,' Richelle said. 'If I don't get home and have a rest soon, I think I'll die.'

Sunny had ducked into the loo and changed into her running gear so she could run home. There's a girl who loves to sweat! She's a fitness maniac. If she's not running, she's at a gym class. If she's not at gym, she's at tae-kwon-do class

18

learning how to kick people in the teeth (just in self-defence, she says). She only comes up to my shoulder, but she's a dangerous person to know. I wouldn't want her to lose her temper with me.

'Well, what do you think?' Liz asked. 'An hour or two after school every afternoon for one or two people. Who wants it?'

'Not me,' Richelle said. 'That guy is weird! And that shop is really *off*!'

'How about you, Nick?'

'Not my style,' Nick said, coolly.

'Elmo?'

'I'll do it if you want me to but I've got to help Dad on the paper Tuesday and Wednesday.'

'Sunny?'

'I don't like that shop either. I don't mind Mr Sid, or whatever his name is—'

'Foy.'

'—but the place gives me the shivers. It's so dark and stuffy and closed in.'

'And did you *see* the people who live upstairs?' Richelle rolled her eyes.

'Yeah, what's wrong with them?' asked Liz.

'Talk about dags. Especially her. That smock thing she was wearing—yuck!'

'Richelle, she's pregnant, for heaven's sake!'

'That's no excuse for looking like a dag. There are some really good maternity clothes around now.'

'I don't know, Richelle. Sometimes I wonder about you,' Liz sighed. 'But we're not here to talk about that anyway.

We're here to see who wants some work. How about you, Tom?'

I didn't want to seem anxious, but I really wanted to work in the magic shop. Maybe Sid would give me a discount on some of the tricks and stuff.

'I wouldn't mind,' I said casually. 'Dust kind of bothers me sometimes, but that's okay. I think it could be kind of . . . enlightening.'

A couple of the others laughed and, sure enough, I blushed. Why did I have to say 'enlightening' when I just meant it would be fun?

'Tom, you're a real dork, you know that?' Nick said. 'That place is about as enlightening as a funeral parlour.'

'I'll do it,' I said.

'What days?' Liz asked.

'I don't know, every weekday, I guess.'

'You can't,' Liz said. 'The agreement is that we only work three days maximum. I'll do two days and you can do three. We each work two hours.'

'Suits me.'

'If there's anything that needs two people at a time, we can double up,' Liz said. 'It doesn't look like it's going to take that long. We should finish it in a week, like Mr Foy said. You want to start on Monday?'

'Sure,' I said, looking bored. 'May as well.'

The fact is, I could hardly wait.

It was getting dark and I was still hanging around the office giving Elmo a hand trying to get a program to run on the computer, when Zim came out of his office.

'Be careful on your way home, Tom,' he told me. 'The Gripper hit someone again last night, you know. A woman.'

'Where?' I asked.

'Over near Federation Park.'

My house backed Federation Park.

'We were just down that way,' Elmo said, 'at Sid's Magic Shop.'

'The police said the victim had been to the Commonwealth Autobank. She's from the country—just down here for a week, poor woman. Hadn't heard about the Gripper. Apparently he followed her till he knew it was safe to make his move.'

'Is she okay?' Elmo asked.

'Bruised neck, but she didn't want to go to hospital,' Zim said. 'We'll be finishing up in a couple of hours, Tom. Happy to give you a lift then if you want. You can call your mum and tell her you'll be late. I don't like the idea of you walking home on your own in the dark. Not with things as they are.'

'I'll be okay,' I said.

'Yeah, the Gripper only robs people who have money,' Elmo laughed.

Or people he thought were carrying money.

I didn't fancy hanging around for two hours even if I was a bit nervous about walking through Raven Hill in the dark. It was Friday night. I was hungry. I wanted to get home.

'I'll be okay,' I said.

It was somewhere near the post office that I sensed that something was very wrong . . .

21

5

The chase

A few cars passed by and then the streets were quiet. Most
people were home now getting ready for their evening meals,
watching the news on TV, just relaxing after work.

I rounded the corner at the Commonwealth Bank and
the light from the Autobank was shining out into the street.
There was no-one around. Since the Gripper went into
business no-one in Raven Hill was game to take out money
after dark unless they were with someone to stand watch.

About a block further on the streetlights were out. Only
lights from the houses kept the street from total darkness.

Home was near, only about five minutes walk if I took
the short cut through Federation Park or fifteen minutes if I
kept to the street and took the long way around. I'd make the
decision on which way to go when the time came.

I didn't have to decide yet.

In a house I heard a woman yelling at her kids, telling
them to turn the TV down. 'That thing's loud enough to wake
the dead!' she screamed. Her voice alone was loud enough to
wake the dead.

As I crossed the street I heard the slight scuffing sound of a shoe on the footpath behind me. I turned slowly, pretending to look in the windows of a house but really looking back out of the corner of my eye.

There was nothing there.

I started humming a tune and tried to remember where I'd heard it. It was one of those songs that gets stuck in your head and you automatically start singing or humming it every few minutes even when you try not to. Song pollution.

The scuffing came again. This time I turned quickly to see if there was someone behind me.

There was.

A shape crossed the footpath and disappeared up a driveway beside a darkened house. Someone going home? It was a man, I was pretty sure of that from the way he moved. But how can you really tell?

Somehow just seeing the figure made me feel better. I relaxed a little. It wasn't a ghost or a creature, it was a real person, someone taking in a rubbish bin or checking the letterbox.

He wasn't coming after me. It wasn't the Gripper.

I turned into Riley Street. I'd have to make a decision soon. The path through the park was only half a block along now. The streetlights were on and most of the houses had lights on in them.

Plenty of light.

If I was sure no-one was following me I'd duck down through the park and be home in no time at all. Federation Park isn't very big. You'd be able to see the back of our house from the entrance if there weren't bushes and trees in the way.

If anything was suspicious, I'd just keep walking around

the block and come in from the front. Ten more minutes, that's all. And there'd be houses all along the way and plenty of people to hear me if I yelled for help.

But I didn't want to give in to the fear.

I stopped and looked around. There was no-one in sight.

No problems.

No-one following me.

I stood there near the short cut for a whole minute, looking around, peering in through the trees, listening for any sign of movement. Nothing. Not a thing. My stomach rumbled. If it had been some mad murderer running around Raven Hill killing people then I wouldn't have gone in there.

But the Gripper wasn't a murderer—not yet, anyway.

He was a robber, a man who followed people who he thought had money in their pockets until he could get them alone. Usually women on their own.

I wasn't a woman.

I didn't have more than a couple of bucks on me.

He wouldn't want me.

I turned quickly and plunged down onto the dirt path and into the bushes. In a minute I was in the clearing where the play equipment was. Ahead I could see the dark silhouettes of the pine trees that guarded the little bridge across the gully. Home was a hop, step and jump from the bridge. Everything was fine. I turned once or twice to make sure I wasn't being followed.

I began humming again and remembered where the tune came from. It was from a TV toilet-paper commercial. How embarrassing. Don't want to get caught humming that at school.

I was laughing to myself when I heard the twig break.

24

I looked around quickly. Nothing moved. Maybe it was an animal. Maybe it wasn't.

The moon came out from behind a cloud and I could see the path better now. I started jogging and then heard the thud of footsteps somewhere behind me, somewhere in the distance.

Then I was running and the footsteps behind me were running too, coming up fast. I turned quickly but looked back, afraid I'd hit a tree.

There was a man behind me and he was on the path, pelting towards me, gaining on me with every step.

I thought he was shouting at me as he ran, I heard a word—a couple of words—but I couldn't be sure with my blood pounding in my head, my lungs straining for air.

Who was he? Why was he chasing me? It couldn't be the Gripper. It couldn't!

This isn't happening, I thought.

I had my hands out in front of me, barely making out the path, hitting a bush and the side and bouncing back to it.

Please, please let me outrun him.

Now I could see the glint of the moon shining on the handrails of the bridge. If I could only hurl myself between them I'd be across in four strides and then through the fence into my backyard. If I called for help now, someone might hear me. But if I yelled it might make him even angrier.

He might slit my throat just to stop my screaming and he'd be away, blending into the darkness of the trees, before help came.

My feet slapped the boards of the bridge. Nearly, nearly . . .

A figure loomed up in front of me, blocking my path.

6

Words words words

I yelled. A torch glared into my eyes.

'Police,' barked the figure, and by then his partner was standing behind me.

I nearly collapsed with relief. 'Oh,' I said, gasping for breath. 'I thought . . . you were him.'

The police, of course, thought I was the Gripper.

They didn't get rough or anything, but I guess you couldn't blame them for being suspicious. I mean, they really didn't know what the guy looked like. I guess he couldn't have been young like me. But I'm tall, and in the dark they weren't about to take any chances.

They asked who I was and everything and they wrote it down. I didn't have any identification on me. I told them where I lived. OK, they said, and off we went. Weren't Mum and Brian surprised!

My half-brothers—that's Mum's and Brian's kids— thought it was really great me coming home with the police and everything. Mum talked to the cops about me and asked what was happening about finding the Gripper, but she didn't use that name because she didn't want Adam and Jonathon to know what was happening. She said something like, 'Do you have any clues about the guy?' She just called him 'the guy'.

'I'm afraid not,' one of the cops said.

Adam's only five years old but he made this incredible face.

'Jack the Gripper!' he yelled. 'Tom's Jack the Gripper!'

You had to laugh—and we all did, even Brian.

○

Once the cops were out of the way, it was lecture time. Brian is big on lectures. I guess it's because he's a teacher or something.

'Ron Larson tells me you were entertaining his class today,' he said.

'Yeah,' I said.

I try to keep my answers short when Brian starts one of his lectures. It's useless trying to tell him your side of the story because he's always right. Arguing with Brian is like putting more wood on a fire. Just keeps him going.

'You know, you're a good lad, Tom,' he said, 'but you'll never get anywhere just being a good lad.'

'I know,' I said.

(Always best to agree with him.)

'You can't go through life being a comedian, Tom. Even comedians have to plan their lives. They have to take things seriously sometimes. They have to work hard at what they do.'

'Yes,' I said.

'The best ones study their craft intensely. You can bet your boots they take that studying seriously too. They know it's going to be their bread and butter some day.'

'Yes,' I said.

'Don't you think it's time you started thinking about your bread and butter, Tom?'

'Yes.'

Brian wasn't like my real dad. Dad would have at least given me a chance to explain. Not Brian. I mean, sure I got in trouble with Mr Larson but it wasn't any big deal. Everything was a big deal with Brian—especially when something happened at school.

'There were these two boys I taught in high school many years ago,' he went on. 'This wasn't in Raven Hill. They were both bright boys who could have really gone places. One of them listened in class and saved his jokes for when he was with his mates. The other one just couldn't help himself. He was always trying to be the class clown. He mucked up all the time. And you know what?'

Go ahead, tell me, I thought. The one who mucked up got killed by a terrorist when he made a joke about the guy's hand grenades, and the other one is the prime minister.

'Are you listening to me, Tom?'

'Yes,' I said.

'The one who saved his humour for the appropriate moment went on to become a lawyer. Now he has a wife, three beautiful children, and a lovely home in a good suburb. He's set for life.'

'How about the other one?' I asked.

'He started university but he dropped out. Couldn't apply himself, I guess. Last I heard he was working on a ship, cleaning decks and polishing brass. He was sailing around

South America somewhere. He's nobody, going nowhere. But he could have really been someone, Tom, if he had only kept himself under control.'

Mum was fiddling with knives and forks on the table. She looked over at me and frowned. You could tell she didn't like Brian's lecture either, but as usual she wasn't game to say anything. I sometimes wonder if she thinks she might lose another husband if she says what she thinks to Brian. Big loss.

'You mean,' I said, 'that if only the comedian had listened and not mucked up he could be living in a posh suburb and going to the office every day in a suit. Right?'

'The day will come when you wish you could do that too,' said Brian. 'Mark my words. There's still time, Tom, if you pull your socks up. You're a talented boy. You could make a valuable contribution to society.'

Valuable contribution to society! That lawyer probably makes his money keeping gangsters from going to gaol. Big contribution to society. But you can't talk about these things to Brian. I mean, what good does Brian do anyone? He teaches ancient history to a few kids and then comes home and sits in front of the TV and drinks beer.

'When they catch this Gripper guy,' Brian said, 'and look into his background, I'll bet your bottom dollar they'll find that he was once just an ordinary kid like you who couldn't apply himself.'

An ordinary kid like me? I liked that.

'Now he's ripping off strangers because he's bitter about his failure, and it's the only way he knows of to get rich,' Brian added.

Why was Brian always so depressing? What a difference

from Dad. Dad used to be an architect but he stopped and became a painter. Now he lives over on the coast in Banyan with Fay. She's an artist too. Neither of them makes much money, but they like they way they live and that's all that matters to them.

I've heard Brian talking to Mum about Dad. Of course he thinks Dad's a failure. I heard him say that Dad wasted a lot of taxpayers' money going to uni.

'What I'd like you to do, Tom,' Brian said, 'is to make yourself a promise right now. I want you to promise yourself that you'll take your studies more seriously starting right now.'

'OK.'

'OK, what?'

'I will.'

'Say it,' Brian persisted. 'Say, I promise—myself—that I won't be the class clown any more.'

'Why do you want me to say it out loud? I mean it's a promise to myself, isn't it?'

'This way you won't forget. Say it.'

This time he'd gone too far. I didn't want to get in a fight but I wasn't about to let him do this to me either.

Adam and Jonathon were arguing over the TV controls while all this was going on. They were good kids—considering they were *his* kids. Heaven help them when they got older and had to make promises to themselves for Brian's sake!

I started thinking about the sailing comedian. I reckon he started his own comedy club in Rio, got rich and famous and now he's the president of Brazil. That's what I'd like to think anyway. Or maybe he's just lying on a beach somewhere telling jokes to the seagulls and having a good time.

'Well, Tom?' Brian asked.

Now I could feel my head heating up and I knew I wasn't blushing. I was getting really angry and I knew what I had to do—get away.

I stood up and headed for my room.

'It's time to think very seriously about your life, Tom,' he called after me. 'It really is.'

Some day I was going to start thinking very seriously about a life a long way away from Brian and Raven Hill.

South America here I come!

7

Teen Power
overload

We were having a very quiet dinner. Brian wasn't talking to me and Mum wasn't talking, full stop. Only Adam and Jonathon were talking and I guess they were making up for the rest of us.

The phone rang and I picked it up.

'Just got a phone call from a lady,' Liz told me. 'It's a child-minding job. Baby-sitting, okay?'

'Why not?' I said.

'Just one kid but his mother wants two of us at a time, every weekday from three-thirty to five-thirty for two weeks. She's willing to pay double our usual fee.'

'Double because there's two people or double double?'

Brian gave me this really hard have-her-call-back-after-dinner look and I ignored it.

Mum had her hands full helping Jonathon and trying to convince Adam that people who never eat vegetables stay five for the rest of their lives. Well, that's not exactly what she was telling him but it might just as well have been.

'Double double,' Liz said. 'She wants two of us and she's willing to pay us *each* double.'

'What's the catch?' I asked.

'None that I know of. Well, we're supposed to take him out, like walking around or something. We can take him to our own houses if we want. She doesn't want him cooped up in her place all the time, which is fair enough.'

'Everybody's going to want this one,' I said.

'Yeah, I know. It could cause problems.'

'Where does she live?' I asked. Maybe that was the catch.

'Her name's Mrs Anderson,' said Liz. 'She lives in that block of flats behind Sid's Magic Shop. There's an empty block and then there's the flats. You know?'

'Anderson?' I asked. 'What's the kid's name?'

'Tarquin.'

That was the catch.

'Hold on!' I said. '*Tarquin Anderson*? Did you say, Tarquin Anderson?'

'Yes. He's a real little—'

'He's a real little one all right. No way, Liz. That kid's a monster.'

'He can't be all that bad.'

'He is, Liz! The kid's impossible. It would take four of us—one to hold each arm and leg—to control that kid. You look after him if you want to, but I don't want anything to do with him.'

'His mother told me he was shy. She said he was very sensitive.'

'Shy? Sensitive? The kid's only been in Raven Hill for six months and I reckon he's already got a criminal record.'

'Tom, he's only seven! You make him sound like a gang of Hell's Angels or something. She says that he's very creative and she wants to make sure he has a chance to express his creativity.'

'Liz, he's in Jonathon's class. He steals everything that's not nailed down. He's a bully and a con man. He's creative all right but not the way his mother thinks. Jonathon come over here and tell Liz about Tarquin Anderson.'

Jonathon jumped down from the table and came to the phone.

'Hey! Where are you going, young man?' Brian called.

'It's important,' I said. 'It'll just take a sec.'

God I wish that man would just relax for a second. Did he think his kid was going to starve to death?

I handed the telephone to Jonathon.

'Hello . . . yes?' he said. 'Tarquin showed his bottom . . . No, his bottom . . . to cars . . . yes, lots of things . . . no. I don't know.'

'Tell her about all the other stuff he gets up to at school,' I whispered. But it was no use. Jonathon was listening without saying anything. He's a real little talker usually but give him a telephone and he clams up.

'I'll take it, Jonno,' I said, grabbing the phone and sending him back to the table.

'I'll tell you later, Liz,' I said in a low voice. 'The point is, the kid's uncontrollable. This is a job we ought to turn down.'

'It's only for two weeks,' Liz said. 'What could go wrong?'

'What,' I asked, 'after he burns our houses down? Well, I suppose he could always kill us.'

'What's got into you?' Liz asked. 'Where's the jokey, jolly lad?'

'Sorry. I guess I'm just all joked out,' I said. 'But I really don't want the job myself.'

'I can only do two days because of Miss Plummer, delivering the *Pen* and cleaning the magic shop. But the others'll love the chance to make that much money,' Liz said. 'OK, let's meet at the Glen tomorrow morning at ten. We'll work it out then, okay?'

'Rightio.'

'You ring Sunny and Elmo and I'll contact the others.'

Liz was right about me not being myself.

I knew it, and so did Mum. She had a talk to me later in my room and asked if I wanted to visit Dad in the holidays. She didn't realise that the real reason I was on edge wasn't Brian or school or anything—it was the Gripper. After the chase with the cops I just didn't seem to be able to get the guy out of my head.

Maybe I knew then what would finally happen . . .

8

The plan

'What's this about bare bottoms?' Nick asked me. 'Is this another one of your jokes?'

The others were all waiting there at the Glen when I arrived.

'That Tarquin kid,' I said. 'My little brother said he was dropping his trousers to passing cars right in front of the school.'

'So you reckon that if he doesn't murder us he'll embarrass us to death, is that right?'

'You do what you want,' I said. 'I'm staying right out of this one.'

'OK,' said Liz, 'who wants some of the baby-sitting and to earn a fortune?'

'Me!' said Nick.

'And me,' said Richelle.

'And me,' said Elmo.

'Sunny told me she wants to do some too,' Liz said, looking over at Sunny who was pulling out pen and paper from her bag. 'I don't mind helping if Tom doesn't mind doing the magic shop on his own.'

'No, that's fine with me,' I said. 'I'll work the whole five days.'

Of course I liked the idea of working in the magic shop, but I also liked the idea of seeing less of Brian for a while.

'We're only supposed to work three days a week,' Liz said doubtfully. 'Still, just this once . . . Sure your mum won't mind?'

'Nope,' I said. I crossed my fingers.

'Remember, you've got the *Pen* delivery before school on Thursday as well. This could cut into your study time. No big assignments due?'

'Nope.'

'Tom doing homework!' Elmo said. 'You wouldn't read about it.'

'Well, you will,' I said. 'When you learn how to read, that is.'

'OK,' said Liz. 'Everyone wants a piece of the babysitting except Tom. Two people at a time. Elmo's busy Tuesday and Wednesday. I'm busy Friday. Richelle's got dancing class. Sunny's got gym and tae-kwon-do. We've got that dog-walking every day—um . . .' She frowned in concentration. 'So that means . . .'

'You and Elmo do Tarquin Anderson on Monday,' interrupted Sunny, who'd been quietly working it out on a piece of paper. 'And Richelle walks the dog. Richelle and Nick do Tarquin on Tuesday, and I walk the dog . . .'

Her calm voice went on. She had it all organised. She'd thought of everything. Liz sat back in relief. So did I. My five afternoons at the magic shop were safe.

'Is that okay with everyone?' Liz asked, after Sunny had finished. 'You've all got three afternoons' work a week except Tom, who has five. I've got four. That's all right. This is an emergency. Now look, no changes unless they're absolutely necessary, or we'll get into a mess. OK?'

'Aye, aye, sir,' Nick said, saluting.

○

Sunny had jogged to the Glen. It was cool so she was wearing her winter running gear. When everyone else left I asked her if she minded if I did a sketch of her.

'Sure,' she said, 'but make it really quick because I have to visit my great-grandmother.'

'I'm the quickest draw in this here town, pardner,' I said, pulling out a pencil and opening my sketch pad. 'Just sit on the grass facing me. I'm only going to do your face, okay?'

Sunny's a good mate. I always feel safe with her—even if her mother *is* our family doctor.

Her father's Roy Chan, a quite famous American tennis player. He and Sunny's mother split up years ago and he moved back to the States to work as a coach. I guess the divorce thing makes Sunny and me feel like we have something in common that the others wouldn't understand.

Sunny's dad's re-married but her mum hasn't. Sometimes Sunny worries that she's lonely—as if that were possible with patients yakking at her all day and five daughters raving on all night!

'She should marry again, too,' Sunny says. 'But she says there aren't any good men around.'

'She can have Brian,' I tell her.

'Thanks, but no thanks,' she says.

Sunny's no fool.

○

'How's the drawing coming?' Sunny asked after a while. 'I've really got to go.'

'It's okay,' I said, 'but it would be easier if you grew a beard.'

Why do I say these stupid things?

'Am I that ugly?' Sunny asked.

Of course Sunny has a really nice face and I wanted to say so, but I just couldn't.

'No,' I said. 'It's just easier to draw faces that have lots of lines and moles and beards and that.'

I showed her the drawing and she seemed to like it so I gave it to her. Then I told her about the police chasing me last night. I didn't tell her how scared I was. I made it sound funny.

We started talking about the Gripper. She said she wasn't worried because she reckoned she could out-run him.

'Did you hear about the woman he tried to rob last night?' I asked.

'Another one!'

'Yeah. She was putting out her rubbish bin. Like, the street was really dark because the streetlights were out. She was in her underwear and she decided that nobody would see her so she just went out to the footpath in her underwear.'

'What!?'

'Yeah. In her underwear. The Gripper came up and grabbed her from behind but she got away.'

'How'd she do that?'

'She gave him the slip.'

'How?'

'The slip. Get it? Her slip. She gave him the slip?'

'Oh you!' she said and then she burst out laughing.

I knew there was another reason Sunny was a good mate—she laughed at my jokes.

9

Magic magic magic

I usually hate Monday mornings. Come to think of it, I'm not keen on Tuesday, Wednesday, Thursday or Friday mornings either. But this Monday morning I woke up before my alarm went off and was up and dressed in a flash.

The day flew by and after school I headed for the magic shop. Liz and Elmo walked along with me. They were on their way to pick up Tarquin from school. They were going to take him back to Liz's place till Tarquin's mother got home from work.

Elmo told us about the latest Gripper attack. This time it was an old man, a doctor, who was going to someone's house. The Gripper caught him just as he stepped out of the car. He took the doctor's wallet and his medical bag.

'I reckon he was after the drugs,' Elmo said. 'He's got to be a junkie. Why else would he need all that money?'

Elmo had a point.

Nobody mentioned Tarquin. I have to admit I was secretly hoping he'd give them a lot of strife. Nothing too bad, mind you, but if he was a perfect angel it was going to make me look pretty stupid after I'd bad-mouthed the kid.

❁

Sid was there behind the counter when I entered the shop. The laughter from the door nearly made me laugh too.

Sid had his artificial arm on and it had those curved metal pincers on it—sort of like a hook but it wasn't sharp and it opened and closed, if you know what I mean. He was holding a piece of paper and there were lots of little receipts lying in piles in front of him.

There was no-one else in the shop.

'Tax time,' he said.

He slipped his arm into Jacko's back.

'He just loves it when it's tax time,' Jacko said. 'It gives him something to do.'

'That'll be enough, Jacko,' Sid said.

'Tom, did you hear the one about the woman who bought a hat?' Jacko asked me. 'The salesman said, "That'll be twenty-five dollars plus tax." And she said, "Forget the tacks, I'll nail it to my head!" Ha ha ha ha! Get it? "Forget the tacks—"'

'Thank you, Jacko,' Sid said, looking up. 'But I don't think Tom came to hear your corny jokes, did you Tom?' He took his arm out of Jacko's back. 'In fact you probably couldn't even hear it because your ear was blocked.'

With this, Sid reached over the counter and pulled an egg out of my ear.

'Now, that's better, isn't it?'

'Hey!' I said. 'How did you do that?'

Sid had this long, rolling kind of laugh that sounded kind of phoney, but it never failed to make me laugh too. I guess it was something he used in his act to get the audience laughing.

'Nothing to it, my lad,' he said. 'Just a little example of Sigmund the Sorcerer's sleight of hand.'

'He's slight of hand, all right,' Jacko said. (This time Sid didn't bother to put his hand in Jacko or work his mouth.) 'He's so slight of hand he only has one of them. Ha ha ha! That's what I call slight of hand!'

'Now, now, Jacko,' Sid said. 'No hand jokes, please.'

'Sorry, Sid.'

'That's more like it.'

I had to admire Sid. There he was with one arm and one eye and a shop that couldn't have been making a cent. Probably Nick was right, and the only real income he had was from the rent from the upstairs flat.

He must have been a real optimist. Not like me. I like people who always look on the bright side of things—but I don't think I could ever be one. It's interesting, though. Lots of people think I'm always in a good mood because of the jokes and stuff.

Little do they know.

'Ever see the shell game?' Sid asked, putting three plastic cups on the counter. Then he took a furry, red ball out of his pocket and put it next to one of the cups.

'I saw this on TV once,' I said.

'Put the ball under one of the cups.'

I did what he said.

'Now keep both eyes on the cup with the ball under it.'

43

'Which is more than *you* can do, Sid,' Jacko's voice said.

'That'll be enough, Jacko.'

'Sorry, Sid.'

Sid slid the cups around the counter one at a time, very slowly and then lined them up again in a row. I didn't have any trouble keeping track of the cup I'd chosen. I made sure he didn't push the cup towards the edge of the counter to let the ball fall to the floor.

'You think it's under this one, don't you?' he said getting ready to lift the one on the right end of the row.

'No,' I said, pointing to the one in the middle. 'It's under that one.'

'That's funny,' he said, lifting the end cup, 'I was sure . . .'

Sure enough, the red ball was under the end cup. Then he lifted the cup on the other end and there was another red ball. Finally, he lifted the one in the middle and there was another red ball.

'Goodness!' he exclaimed. 'Where are they all coming from. They must be breeding in the dark or something.'

How did he do it? I have no idea. Sid just gave me a big smile and said in his Jacko voice, 'It's magic! Do you believe in magic, Tom?'

For the moment I did. At least I wanted to.

'But you're probably itching to get stuck into that storeroom,' he said. 'When you have some time I'll teach you a few of the tricks of the magic trade.'

'Do you mean it?' I asked.

'Of course I do,' he answered. 'Now about the storeroom . . .'

'What about it?'

'I have a confession to make. I don't even know what's in there. I'm about the world's most forgetful and disorganised person. And on top of that I hate throwing stuff away—I save everything. So I'm going to leave it to you. Have a good look around in there and give me your advice, okay?'

10

Puzzle porridge

I spent the next hour just looking through the junk in the storeroom. Well, it wasn't all junk.

There was everything in there: games that weren't selling, old books on how to do magic tricks, broken dress dummies from when the place had been a clothes shop, an old fridge, pieces of a car engine. You name it, it was in there. Piles and piles of it.

'Your considered opinion, sir,' Sid said. 'The easiest thing would be to just turf the lot, wouldn't it be? Take it out in the back lane and leave it for the garbos.'

'I wouldn't,' I said. 'There's a lot of good stuff in there: things you could fix up and sell in the shop or just put ads in the *Pen* and sell. You could even have a sale.'

'Spoken like a true collector. Your room at home isn't as messy as this by any chance?'

He wasn't wrong about that. At least I'm sure Mum would have agreed with him.

'I don't like to waste things if someone else can use them. And why throw away money?'

'What would you keep?'

'Well there's a pile of old masks. I reckon I could clean them up and they'd still be good. You could sell them cheap. And jigsaw puzzles. There's a pile of them. I opened the boxes and they looked okay. It's just that someone cut the tape and opened them. We can tape them closed again, can't we?'

'Oh, them. I'm afraid they're not okay. You see there's a little kid who used to come in here. He never bought anything. He just played around quietly down behind the shelves. Muggins here let him do it. I didn't twig that he was up to something. Then one day a customer returned a jigsaw puzzle because there were pieces missing. Fair enough. There weren't just pieces missing, there were other pieces from other puzzles mixed in. That little so-and-so scrambled all the puzzles!'

'What a—'

'And that's not all. When he finished with that he did the same with the games: the wrong dice in the wrong boxes, things like that. And *that's* not all. He mixed up some of the powders in the make-up kits and then he cut the legs off some of those rubber spiders. That little nipper must have cost me a bomb.'

'Did you tell his parents?'

'Yes, and they offered to pay but I didn't know how much to ask. Besides, I felt partly to blame because I'd let him get away with it. So I said, "Just please don't let him come in the shop ever again." And do you know what his mother said?'

'What?'

'She said he was a very creative child. "Creative!" I said. "If he's creative now I just hope he never gets to be destructive." '

47

'Tarquin Anderson,' I sighed.

'How did you know?'

'He's got a certain reputation,' I said.

I put the puzzles aside and looked through the magic sets. One of them had three magic wands and no rope for the rope tricks. Another box was filled with just bits of rope. All the instruction books were in a third box. I sorted things out and Sid got out his heat-sealer and sealed each set in plastic so it looked like it was new.

'I'll mark these down,' Sid said. 'That way if there's still anything wrong with them people won't feel they've been cheated. Got to keep the customers happy. Don't want to drive them away.'

Then he said in his Jacko voice. 'I used to make a lot of money driving customers away.'

'You did? How'd you do that?'

'I was a taxi driver! Ha ha ha ha.'

'That'll be enough of your corny jokes, Jacko,' Sid said.

There was another thing I liked about Sid besides his cheeriness and his optimism. He had a shop to look after and a living to make and he had to do his tax and all that, but all the same he just wasn't like the other adults I knew. You could just talk to him the way you talk to one of your mates. It was like he was sort of half kid. Like you didn't have to pretend with him.

I got a bucket of soapy water and started cleaning a pile of old rubber masks: Dracula, the Frankenstein monster, and

48

just plain horrible faces. Some were so old that they cracked and tore when I washed them and I had to throw them away.

Behind the masks I found a box of itching powder.

'You can have it, Tom,' Sid said. 'Nobody buys things like that any more.'

'Thanks,' I said, slipping it into my pocket. 'I'll find a use for it.'

'Now unless you want to spend the night with the mice, you'd better get yourself cleaned up and go home.'

The two hours had gone by so fast that it seemed like only half an hour! When I came out of the storeroom it didn't look much better than it had when I started. Sid was back to working on his tax. He handed me an envelope with my two hours' pay.

'It isn't much,' he said. 'But you earned every cent of it.'

'I'm afraid I didn't make much of a hole in the mess,' I said. 'I hope I can finish it all in one week.'

'Don't you worry about that,' he said. 'Things take time. You want to get anything done in life, you've got to be prepared to work and be patient.'

It was the same sort of thing that Brian might have said, but coming from Sid, somehow it sounded okay.

'See you tomorrow,' he said.

And that's when I heard the screams.

11

The terror of Tarquin

The screams were coming from behind the shop. I ran back through the storeroom and peered out the filthy window into the lane. There in the semidarkness were Liz and Elmo each pulling the screaming Tarquin along by his arms. With their other hands they were clutching bits of clothing.

Tarquin was naked except for his underpants.

'I don't want to go home!' he screamed. 'Don't take me home. I'll kill you! I'll kill you!'

I burst out laughing.

Sid looked up again from his work as I passed the counter again. 'Did I hear a familiar voice?' Sid called out.

'You did,' I said. 'Two of the gang—Liz and Elmo—are baby-sitting him.'

'Oh, lucky them.'

❂

That night I carried all seven jigsaw puzzles home with me

and took them to my room. Brian was too busy watching the news to notice and Mum was in the kitchen. Good thing.

Anyway I cleared everything off the floor and dumped the puzzles into seven separate piles. Seven one-thousand-piece puzzles all mixed up together. Seven thousand pieces! This was going to be fun.

As I worked away on them I kept laughing to myself about Tarquin. I wanted to phone Liz and ask her about it but I wanted to see her face.

After a while there was a knock at the door. I don't know how you can tell from a knock, but I knew straightaway it was Jonathon.

'I'm busy,' I said.

I could hear Mum calling out to him to leave me alone because I was studying.

'Can I come in?' Jonathon asked.

'I'm busy.'

'I want to come in.'

'What do you want?'

'I want to tell you a joke.'

Most of the pieces in the pile I was working on were from a jigsaw puzzle of a zoo. I was busy picking out odd bits that belonged to one of the Milky Way.

'Tell me, then,' I said. The least I could do was encourage his sense of humour. His father certainly wouldn't.

There was a silence and then Jonathon said, 'The robber is joking people.'

'What?'

I opened the door and pulled him into the bedroom.

'Don't say anything about the puzzles,' I said. 'Now what are you on about?'

'You know the robber?' he asked.

I guess they must have been talking about Jack the Gripper even in Raven Hill Primary School.

'Yes, I've heard about him.'

'Well, he's killing people with jokes,' Jonathon giggled, and looked at me expectantly.

It was a joke that was going around his school. Jonathon didn't understand it so he wasn't telling it right. I had to put it back together like a jigsaw puzzle. This was it: Did you hear that the Gripper has become a comedian? Now he's *joking* people to death. (Joking, choking—get it?)

'Good one, Jonathon,' I said. 'Keep working on it.'

I filed it away in my brain to tell at school the next day.

I ran to catch up with Liz the next morning, just as she was going into Brian's history class. I tried to keep a straight face, but when she turned and I saw the scratches on her face it wasn't easy.

'Any trouble with Tarquin?' I murmured.

She gave me this really dirty look like she didn't want to talk about it.

'I was just wondering,' I said.

'Oh, shut up, Tom. It's not funny,' she snapped.

'Touchy, touchy.'

By lunchtime everybody in the school knew what happened. Tarquin had been okay on the way to Liz's house.

When he got there he decided he wanted to make pancakes. When Elmo tried to talk him out of it he went off his brain. He smashed every egg in the fridge, threw flour all over the carpets and, while Elmo and Liz were cleaning up, he fed a whole chocolate cake to Liz's dog.

When it was time to go home, Tarquin refused to go. He said he wanted to live at Liz's house for the rest of his life. The only way Elmo and Liz could get him out the door was to tell him they were taking him to play on some swings. There was a little park near his flat so they took him there.

When they got there he started running around in circles saying that he wasn't going home ever again. Then he climbed up this really tall tree and started stripping off and throwing his clothes all over the place. Liz and Elmo finally talked him into coming down but Liz had to climb up and get the clothes that were stuck in the branches.

'She insisted,' Elmo told Sunny. 'I was for leaving the clothes up there and letting his mother go after them.'

In English I drew a cartoon of Tarquin in his underpants and Liz and Elmo pulling him along the street. I gave him this huge mouth. Then I made up a poem and wrote it underneath. It went like this:

'A shy little fellow named Tarquers
Went off to have fun in the park—ers
He climbed up a tree
Then he yelled, "Look at me!"
And he took off his clothes and went starkers.'

Not bad except for the bit about park and park-ers. Well I'm not Shakespeare, am I?

I held it out for Liz to see and she squinted over at it and then looked away again like she didn't even see it. She was really, really cheesed off.

She turned back and said, 'Sometimes you go too far, Tom!'

She was probably right and I felt kind of bad about rubbing it in. I tried to make everything okay at recess.

'So what did Mrs Anderson say when you got back to her place?' I asked.

'She was just worried because it was after dark and because of all the robberies and stuff.'

'Liz,' I said, 'I've got one piece of advice.'

'What's that?'

'Drop him. He's too much trouble.' No sooner were the words out of my mouth when I thought: Ooops! What if they give up baby-sitting for Tarquin and they all want to share my magic shop job?

Luckily Liz said, 'Nick and Richelle have him this afternoon. Nick's not worried about it. He says they'll keep Tarquin in line. He reckons Elmo and I were too soft on him.'

'What's he going to do, glue the kid's clothes on?' I asked.

12

Tom the prestidigitator

That afternoon at the shop, Sid kept telling me to take breaks so he could show me how to do more magic tricks. And he was paying me by the hour. I reckon Nick was right about Sid not being a very good businessman. But I was having a great time!

He showed me how to make things disappear. It was usually the same trick: you took a coin, for example, and while you were talking about what you were about to do you passed it from one hand to the other very casually. Of course you didn't really put it in the other hand.

He was wearing his artificial arm, so he put the coin in the pincers at the end and then pretended to pass it to the other hand. It didn't work, of course, because you could still see where the coin was.

'It helps to have two hands,' Jacko said.

I couldn't help laughing whenever Jacko said anything. He had a really quick, funny way of saying things. It was kind of sick, because I was laughing at Sid having only one hand, but of course it was Sid who was making the jokes.

It was really strange, eerie almost—like there were two people there in the shop, with different personalities. Maybe good ventriloquists really do develop double personalities after a while.

Anyway, Sid went on explaining the disappearing coin trick to me.

'The audience isn't expecting anything,' Sid explained, 'because they don't think the trick has started. They're still waiting for you to do whatever it is that you're going to do and, actually, you've already done it.'

'Like, the coin's already in the wrong hand,' I said.

'Exactly. From there you can quietly drop it in your pocket and get it out of the way. Then you just pretend to throw it up in the air with your empty hand and, of course, there's nothing there. Magic.'

I tried the trick a couple of times but it didn't look very convincing.

'Practice, my boy. Practice,' Sid said. 'I'll turn you into my apprentice in the art of prestidigitation yet.'

'The art of what?'

'Prestidigitation. Presto, fast. Digits, fingers. Fast fingers. The art of fast fingers. Conjuring. Magic tricks have everything to do with making people believe what isn't true. Lying with your hands. But of course the fun of it is the window-dressing, the way you make the tricks *look*. And the jokes. Humour has a lot to do with the fun. I know you're a man who likes a joke.'

'Yeah, I do,' I said. 'I'm afraid I waste a lot of time telling jokes.'

'Rubbish! Making people laugh is never a waste of time, Tom. Sigmund the Sorcerer loved a good joke and everybody loved Sigmund the Sorcerer.'

Then he said in Jacko's voice: 'What do you get when you drop a sorcerer on a landmine?'

'I give up,' I said.

'A flying sorcerer. Ha ha ha! Get it? A flying sorcerer—a flying saucer. Sorcerer. Saucer. Ha ha ha.'

'That'll be enough of that, Jacko,' Sid said.

'It must have been great being a magician and travelling all around the place,' I said.

'It was. I loved it. And I got to be pretty well known, especially in the country areas. Just between you and me it wasn't the best-paying job in the world. Sometimes I'd get a big crowd and sometimes it was rainy and cold and nobody would come. It was a gamble, really. But life's not much fun if it isn't a gamble, I always say. You'll never get what you want if you don't take a chance.'

Bit by bit I was getting the storeroom cleaned out. There was a huge heap of rubbish now in the laneway out behind the old wooden fence. There were lots of things that couldn't be fixed—like two dozen legless spiders—but I convinced Sid to put some other things that were only a little bit damaged into a bin with a sign that said:

EVERYTHING $1.

Once I'd cleared away a lot of the stuff I found the equipment that Sigmund the Sorcerer had used in his act, like a box for sawing someone in half and a lot of juggling rings and balls. And there were some beaut old posters of Sid. One of them had him in a black cape and top hat and in the other one he was wearing a white suit and a red turban.

'You can't throw this out,' I said.

'Why not?' he said. 'It's no good to me now.'

'Can I have it?'

'What? That old stuff? Certainly not. Your mother would be down on me like a tonne of bricks if I let you clutter up her house with my junk.'

It probably would have been Brian and not Mum, but he was right of course.

'You could keep them. There'll be plenty of room when I get this cleared away,' I said hopefully.

'Remember the fire regulations, Tom,' he said. 'I say, turf the lot. We can't have this place going up in smoke just because some sentimental old bloke wants to hang on to his past. Now get yourself tidied up and get out of here.'

I felt really sad for old Sid. Now I knew him better I could see that he hid his real feelings a lot of the time. Just like I did. He acted like he didn't care, but underneath it all you could tell that he did. He cared a lot.

13

Good news, bad news

That night Sunny rang. She was busting to tell me what had happened to Nick and Richelle when they looked after Tarquin.

'Which do you want first: the good news or the bad news?' she asked me.

'Give me the bad news,' I said gleefully.

'No, I'll give you the good news: they managed to keep Tarquin's clothes on. That's about the only good part.'

'How about the bad news?'

Sunny giggled.

'He painted Nick's house.'

'Painted his house? The whole house?'

'No, silly. Let me tell you. They picked him up from school and took him to Nick's place. Nick wanted to show Richelle some videos he'd made.'

'I didn't know Nick had a video camera.'

'Oh, Nick's got everything,' Sunny said. 'OK, so they get to the house and Nick's mother isn't home. Nick warns

59

Tarquin not to get up to anything if he knows what's good for him. He says he isn't going to take any nonsense. He says he'll give Tarquin a dollar if he's good.'

Typical Nick, I thought. Money's always the answer with him.

Sunny went on. 'So Nick starts showing Richelle the videos, and they don't realise anything's wrong till they turn around and see bubbles coming out of the aquarium—like, masses of soap bubbles foaming up and going all over the floor. Tarquin's squirted detergent in the water.'

'You're joking!'

'And then—'

'The house painting,' I reminded her.

'Then,' Sunny continued, 'after Nick has rescued the fish that haven't died, he puts Tarquin in a bedroom with some books and tells him to stay there or die. Then he and Richelle start cleaning out the fish tank. By the time they've finished it's time to take Tarquin home. So they go to get him.'

I could hear Sunny take a breath and start to giggle again.

'There he is, still sitting on the bedroom floor where they'd left him. But then they see there's paint on his shirt. "What's this?" Nick says. And after a while they work out that the kid's climbed out the window and found a tin of paint and some brushes in the garage. More mess, thinks Nick. But it isn't till they go outside that they see what Tarquin's actually done. Right across the front of the house, in huge black letters, is: NICK IS A STINK.'

I laughed. Quite a lot. I couldn't help myself. 'Well, the kid's creative all right,' I said finally. 'You've got to give him that. Did they manage to get the paint off?'

'Nick scrubbed it with turps. He got most of it off before his mother came home. I don't think Richelle did much.'

So much for being tough with Tarquin.

'So who has him tomorrow?' I asked.

'Guess.'

'You?'

'And Liz. And he's *not* going home to my place.'

'So what are you going to do with him? Mrs Anderson wants him to get out and be creative.'

'Liz and I reckon we just have to tell Mrs Anderson that we stay at her place or we don't look after the brat. There's just no other way. And we may not be able to do the whole two hours.'

'Why not?'

'Mum doesn't want me coming back after dark.'

'Why not? It's only just getting dark when you finish.'

'The Gripper, what else?'

'But as long as you're not alone and you're a kid—'

'Mum was talking to one of the police. Someone else was robbed last night. It was one of the solicitors in the Jubilee Building. He was locking up and the Gripper grabbed him in the doorway. He lost about a thousand dollars.'

'He knows who has money—' I started.

'Let me finish. This guy's still in hospital. He's going to be okay, but they reckon that the Gripper's turning violent. They say that you just can't tell what he'll do next.'

'So what are you going to do?'

'I've got to be in before dark, so Mrs Anderson is just going to have to put up with that or find someone else to look after Tarquin. Anyway, got to go. See you tomorrow.'

✹

I was back in my room when Mum opened the door without warning. There I was in the middle of the floor surrounded by puzzle pieces. She must have thought I was working on my homework.

'Oops! I didn't see that,' she said, holding up a hand in front of her eyes. 'Listen, Tom, about this magic shop work.'

'What about it?'

'Two things: Brian and I don't like the idea of you doing it every day of the week. It's too much, sweetie.'

'But it'll be finished soon,' I protested.

'How soon?'

'A few more days.'

'Is that all?'

'Yes, that's all.'

'OK. And try to be in before dark, okay? This whole Gripper thing's getting scary.'

✹

That night I was lying in bed thinking about Sid and the magic shop. Now that I'd been working there a while I had to admit that Nick was right, Sid couldn't be earning enough to stay in business. If he got two customers in a day, he'd be lucky. How many kids are into magic anyway? Sure, he had some make-up kits and some puzzles and games, but you'd never know that from looking at the place. It looked awful. It looked awful from the outside and awful on the inside.

Suddenly it hit me in a flash. The shop *could* make money. Sid *could* stay in business—if only I could get him to listen to me.

14

The big idea

'Sid,' I said. 'I *know* it'll work. It'll cost a bit of money, but . . .'

'Tom, I can get more games in,' Sid said. 'Don't worry about the money. That's no problem for the moment. But the games I have just aren't selling. What makes you think that more games won't just end up collecting dust on the shelves?'

'First let me fix the front window, okay?'

'If you say so.'

The first thing I did was clear everything out. Most of the boxes and packets were so faded from the sun that you couldn't tell what was in them, anyway. Then I cleaned the window inside and out.

Then I got two of the dress dummies from the storeroom. I dressed one of them in Sid's Sigmund the Sorcerer's clothing: pin-striped pants, a white ruffled shirt and a bow tie, a long black cape and his top hat. He had another outfit with a turban and an all-white suit, but I left that in its box in the storeroom.

Then I set up the people-sawing box and put another dummy in it. There was even a wig to make it look more realistic. An old saw in the dummy's hand and two of Sid's old advertising posters on either side finished the job.

Sid went outside and had a good look at it with me.

'It looks great,' he said. 'You're an artist to your fingertips. I'm afraid I'm just an old one-armed, one-eyed trickster. Making the place look good was never one of my strong points.'

As we were standing there, the man and woman from the upstairs flat came by and then stopped and looked. They were off on their evening walk and had come from the back stairs and then around to the front.

'Giving the place a face-lift?' grinned the man.

The woman giggled nervously, and brushed her limp hair out of her eyes.

'Dave and Donelle,' said Sid, 'I'd like you to meet my apprentice, Tom. He's going to make me a rich man, he tells me. Tom, these are my tenants, Dave and Donelle Dinkley. They never promised to make me rich—and they haven't!'

Donelle giggled again, and darted a look at Dave. I got the impression that Sid made her nervous. Actually, he had that effect on a lot of people. They didn't understand his sense of humour, I guess.

Dave was sort of macho, and didn't look too bright, but he was friendly enough. Donelle seemed nice, too, in a weak, giggly sort of way, but when she shook hands I was afraid I was going to start her having her baby. I mean, she was so big! She was like a walking time-bomb.

I could picture the headline in the *Pen*:

WOMAN HAS BABY ON FOOTPATH
AFTER BOY SHAKES HAND TOO HARD

'Looks good, mate,' said Dave, nodding at my window display. Donelle tugged at his arm. She was obviously anxious to keep moving. Before it got too dark, I suppose.

'Lovely people,' Sid said, as we watched them walk slowly away.

'You'd think they'd be nervous, walking around here at night,' I said.

Sid shrugged. 'She has to have her exercise, I guess. Exercise for pregnant ladies is all the go now, isn't it? And she waits until Dave gets home from work. They think he can handle himself well enough for them both.'

'But the Gripper's really clever,' I said. 'And Dave seems a bit dim to me. I don't think he'd be a match for the Gripper at all.'

I went on watching Donelle lumbering away. 'Let's face it, Donelle couldn't run away from a nasty customer if she was paid to,' I added. 'I think they're taking a big risk.'

Sid paused. 'I guess even the Gripper might draw the line at grabbing a pregnant woman like Donelle, Tom,' he said after a while. 'She's safe, I reckon.'

As we stood there a car drove by and then turned around and came back. A woman and a young boy got out and looked at the window display. Sid waved me inside and we waited until they came in.

'May I help you, madam?' Sid said. 'Sigmund the Sorcerer at your service.'

'I didn't even realise this place was here,' the woman said. 'When did you open?'

'Only five short years ago,' Sid said, winking at me. 'And it seems we're only now getting ready for business.'

Within a few minutes the boy had picked out one of the most expensive magic sets in the shop, along with a rubber Frankenstein monster mask and a snake.

When they were out of the shop, Sid turned to me. 'That's the best sale I've made for weeks! And I owe it to you and your window, Tom.'

'That was just the beginning,' I said. 'You've got to do something about the lighting and the sign's got to be repainted.'

'Yeah—it is peeling, I suppose.'

'And it doesn't say what it should say,' I said.

Sid gave me this very suspicious look.

'What exactly should it say?' he asked.

'It should say: "Sid's Magic and Games".'

'There you go about games again. I told you—'

'Sid, I'm not talking about jigsaw puzzles. I'm talking about fantasy games, adventure-game books, brainteaser games, computer games—that's what kids want.'

'Now hold on, Tom. Computer games? I don't know anything about computer games. I don't know anything about computers, full stop. I still don't know what the difference between software and hardware is—except the kind of hardware you buy at the hardware shop.'

'Hardware is the machines: computers and printers and that. Software is the programs—games and stuff.'

'Don't bother, Tom. I'm an old dog and you can't teach me new tricks.'

'But don't you see,' I pleaded, 'you don't have to know anything about computers. Well, not at first. They're just in boxes like any other games. We'll tell you which ones to get in.'

'We?'

'I know a bit about them and Nick and Sunny know a lot.'

'But there's already a place in town that sells computer games: CompuMart.'

'I've thought about that,' I said. 'But they sell stuff to businesses mostly. They have some games, but only a few. Besides, I reckon kids would much rather come into a place like this and buy.'

'Well you've thought about pretty much everything, Tom. Everything except where I'm going to get the money for all this. I said not to worry about that, but I've been working it out since. I don't know if I can stretch to all this. Those computer games are really expensive. Plus there's the new lighting. It's a big gamble.'

'Life's not much fun if it isn't a gamble,' I reminded him.

Sid let out a long laugh.

'I can see I've got to be careful what I say around here,' he said. 'OK, give me a few days to think about it. In the meantime, let's forget about the grand schemes and princely riches and get some more cleaning done, shall we?'

'You've got it.'

○

Mrs Anderson wasn't happy about Sunny and Liz keeping Tarquin at home. She said she wasn't sure about Teen Power Inc. and would think about getting someone else to mind him. She couldn't understand why they couldn't just play nicely with Tarquin and everybody have a good time.

'He loves to play,' she explained. 'He is going through a bit of a rough patch at the moment, but it's all part of growing up. If there is any damage, my husband and I will be happy to pay for it.'

As Liz said to me later, the Andersons *had* paid for Nick's new fish. But would they be willing to foot the bill for the psychiatric care for Teen Power after Tarquin had wrecked their mental health?

15

Problems

The next day—it must have been Thursday because we all delivered the *Pen* that morning—I arrived at Sid's just in time to see the electricians leaving. There were three new fluorescent tubes lighting the aisles and two spotlights in the window. Sid was all smiles when I came in. Jacko sat on the counter beside him.

'Well I've taken the plunge,' Sid said. 'I just hope it's the right decision.'

'Cost an arm and a leg, Sid,' said Jacko.

'Yes it did, Jacko.'

'You've still got the leg to go, Sid.'

'That'll be enough, Jacko.'

'These'll help pay for it,' I said, showing him the jigsaw puzzles I'd managed to sort out.

Of course we both knew that even if he sold them all it wouldn't come close to paying for even one of the lights.

'I decided it's getting to be sink or swim time,' Sid said. 'I've been treading water for too long. You made me realise that. By the way, I did some planning. I rang some suppliers.'

'Of computer games?'

'Yes, and other games. It's all so high-tech these days. Nothing's cheap any more. When I was a kid we used to have more fun with old tins and bits of wire than you can imagine. These days if kids don't get toys that sing in six languages and stand on their heads they don't want them.'

'You mean, you're really going to get some new games?' I asked excitedly.

'I'll give you a definite maybe on that one, Tom,' he said with a wink. He put his hand up Jacko's back.

'Work first, decisions later,' said Jacko. 'Right, Sid?'

'Right, Jacko.'

One problem with the new lights was that now you could see everything much better—so you could see that the floors and shelves were filthy and the paint on the walls and ceiling was peeling.

I went to work clearing shelves and cleaning them with soapy water. When I took a break Sid showed me how to use a trick magic wand that disappeared and turned into a bunch of coloured scarves.

Actually the scarves came out of the middle of the wand when the wand collapsed. There was a button to push and a spring inside. Once the wand collapsed you were supposed to put it up your sleeve really quickly. I tried lots of times, but I couldn't do it.

'Practice makes perfect,' Sid said. 'Don't worry, we'll turn you into another Sigmund the Sorcerer yet.'

'Don't hold your breath, Sid,' said Jacko.

Just then the Dinkleys came into the shop through the back door.

'Anybody home?' Donelle called, knocking at the side of

71

the door as they came in.

'Enter, enter,' said Sid. 'What can we do for you?'

'Well, um, it's just . . .' Donelle began. She stopped. 'You say it, Dave,' she whispered.

Dave stood there for a minute, fidgeting, and then said, 'Sorry to say it, mate, but we have to leave the flat. We're going Saturday week.'

Sid looked so shocked. He put his hand over his heart as if to check that it was still beating.

'But why?' he asked.

'It's just that Donelle's about due and we have to start looking for a bigger place.'

'A bigger place?' Sid asked. 'Isn't there enough room up there? There are two bedrooms. I don't mind the sound of a baby crying, if that's what you're worried about. I know the flat's not very fancy, but . . .'

Donelle giggled nervously, brushed her hair back and put her hand over her stomach. 'Oh, it's not the flat . . . I mean, there's nothing wrong with the flat, Mr Foy,' she breathed.

Dave put his arm around her. 'To tell the truth, mate, it's just—that I think Donelle's getting a bit—you know—nervous—around here,' he said, looking Sid straight in the eye, man to man.

Sid nodded slowly.

'My mother said she'd have us for a while,' gabbled Donelle. 'Till the baby comes. Then we can find a little place of our own. In the country, maybe. Somewhere nice—and quiet.'

'Oh, I see,' said Sid.

Dave pulled out a small wad of money that he'd already counted.

'This is last month's rent and this month's,' he said, holding it out awkwardly. 'That should take us up to Saturday week.' He paused. 'Sorry about this, mate.'

When Sid didn't take the money, Dave put it down on the counter. Then he and Donelle left, hand in hand, without saying anything else. Sid didn't say anything else either, but after they'd gone he started talking about them, and worrying about why they were leaving.

'You don't suppose all the banging around down here disturbed them, do you?' he asked me.

'I don't think so,' I said.

'Maybe I was charging them too much for their rent. I thought it was pretty low already, really. Still, I think I'll offer to reduce it even more and see if they'll stay on.'

'Sid,' I said, 'I think they just want to move out, that's all. After all, well, you can understand Donelle feeling funny about Raven Hill at the moment, with the Gripper on the loose. Did you hear he mugged three separate people last night? He's never done that before. He's getting greedy.'

Sid was silent for a moment. 'Donelle wouldn't have had anything to worry about,' he said after a moment. 'I'm sure of it. It's obvious that people like the Dinkleys don't have money worth taking, anyway. There's no need for them to be scared of the Gripper.'

'Well, they obviously are,' I said. 'Look, Sid, just forget about the Dinkleys. They're boring, anyway. You can rent the flat to someone else.'

'It's not that easy,' he muttered. 'I don't want just anyone renting above my shop. The Dinkleys were perfect. Perfect.' He was almost talking to himself.

'Nice and quiet and not too nosy,' said Jacko. 'Respectable young couple. Good cover for a villain like you, Sid.'

'That'll be enough, Jacko,' said Sid absent-mindedly. He sighed. 'Well, I can't afford to keep the place empty so I guess I'll have to move back in myself.'

I remembered what Nick had said about the rent from the flat keeping the shop going.

'Is this going to affect the . . . the plan?' I asked. 'The games, and so on?'

He paused. 'No,' he said slowly at last. 'No, it won't affect the plan. I've gone this far. I may as well go the whole way.'

'Sink or swim, Sid?' crowed Jacko.

'Sink or swim, Jacko,' said Sid.

16

Seeds of doubt

When I got to school on Friday morning the kids were all talking about another attack by Jack the Gripper. It had happened the night before. This time the victim was Richelle's aunt.

When she drove into her garage after work he was waiting in there in the dark, so as soon as she got out of the car he grabbed her and pushed her really hard against the side of the car. Then he snatched her handbag and left her counting while he got away.

She was taken to hospital with bruises to her head, but they let her go after an hour or two. Of course, she was really rattled. I looked for Richelle to ask her about it but she hadn't come to school. Some of the kids said that her parents were going to keep her at home till the Gripper was caught.

Liz was worried because it was Richelle's turn, along with Nick, to look after Tarquin that afternoon.

There was a new joke going around. 'Did you hear about the bloke who's going around stealing fish? Jack the Kipper.'

The only problem was that half the kids didn't know that kippers were fish.

At lunch Sunny let me draw a picture of her while she chinned herself on the branch of a tree in the playground. Of course this time I did the whole of her and not just the head, making it as realistic as possible. The only problem was I was taking too long at it.

'Hurry up, hurry up! My arms are giving out!' Sunny complained. 'I thought you were the quickest draw in town!'

I had to finish it with Sunny standing on the ground with her arms up like she was trying to chin herself. Meanwhile, she told me about Tarquin's latest drama.

'Elmo and I decided to take him to the *Pen*. We weren't going to take him inside or anything, it was just somewhere to walk to,' Sunny explained. 'Then, on the way, we heard an ice-cream van playing its stupid tune.'

'Tarquin wanted an ice-cream, of course, but he didn't have any money on him. So Elmo told him that the ice-cream vans only play that song when they're out of ice-cream,' Sunny said with a laugh. 'Tarquin actually believed him but then he saw people buying stuff. Then Elmo told him that it was winter and you couldn't buy ice-cream, you could only order it and they'd deliver it next summer.'

'Did he believe it?'

'No. He saw somebody eating one. Then he picked up a rock and said he was going to throw it at a car if we didn't buy him an ice-cream.'

'So what'd you do?'

'We bought him an ice-cream,' said Sunny glumly. 'What else could we do?'

'The kid is creative,' I said. 'You have to give him that.'

'He was the best he's been so far,' Sunny said. 'Elmo found a way to tame him. He kept asking him questions about everything. Like he was interviewing him for the *Pen*.'

'What kind of questions?'

'Simple ones but not silly ones. Things like, "Do you think kids should be allowed to eat whatever they want?" and "How old do you think someone should be to drive a car?" Things like that.'

'Did he answer them?'

'He did. That boy is *full* of opinions. Elmo just kept him talking. Simple, huh?'

By now a lot of kids were crowding around me watching me draw. Some of them made stupid comments but I knew that most of them were impressed. Sunny didn't say anything, but I think she was getting kind of embarrassed.

Anyway, I finished the drawing and I thought it looked pretty good. Sunny didn't. She didn't think it looked anything like her. People hardly ever *do* think pictures of them *look* like them—not even photographs. Funny isn't it?

I caught Nick just before the bell ended lunch.

'You've got the little house painter on your own today,' I said. 'Unless Richelle turns up. What are you going to do?'

'Richelle's here now. I just talked to her. Everything's under control. Today Tarquin is going to behave himself like never before.'

'Elmo kept him talking and he was okay.'

'I know,' he said. 'I just had a word to him. Tarks and I have this little understanding: he behaves himself and he gets to keep his front teeth.'

'Yeah, sure.'

My grin must have irritated Nick. 'How's the museum going? Got all the exhibits dusted?' he sneered.

'Have you seen the window?'

'What? You reckon cleaning the window's going to do anything?'

'I fixed it up. Have a look. I got some dummies from the back and put Sid's magician's clothes on one—'

'Moysten, please.'

'Don't laugh. It's really bringing in the customers.'

'Pull the other one,' he said. 'If he sells more than a hundred bucks worth of that stuff every week I'll eat that ventriloquist's dummy of his. Come to think of it, I'm surprised *he* hasn't eaten the dummy yet.'

'He's got big plans for the place.'

'Like what?'

'He wants to start selling lots of different sorts of games—game books and computer games and stuff.'

'Really?'

'I suggested it and he liked the idea.'

Nick looked at me very seriously.

'Are you sure?' he asked.

'That's what he says.'

'Well maybe he's not as hopeless as I thought he was,' Nick said slowly. 'But where's he going to get the money?'

I shrugged. I didn't want to talk about Sid's affairs with Nick.

Nick laughed.

'Hey, he's probably going to raise his tenants' rent,' he said. 'They won't thank you for your brilliant idea.'

'The tenants are moving out,' I snapped.

'I'm not surprised,' said Nick. 'I wouldn't want to be bringing up a baby with a weirdo like Sid hanging around downstairs.'

'They're not leaving because of Sid!' I exploded. 'They're leaving, because of the Gripper. They're obviously scared to walk the streets. It's—it's ridiculous!' I could feel myself going red. 'The Gripper's wrecking everyone's lives. Why can't the cops catch him? What's wrong with them?'

Nick stared at me. 'Calm down, Moysten,' he said. 'The Gripper's not your problem. He's not likely to hit you, is he?'

'But why can't they catch him?' I raved on. It was as though once I'd started talking, I couldn't stop. 'He can't just disappear into thin air, like they say. No-one can run that fast. Someone must see him getting away after these muggings.'

Nick shrugged. 'Well no-one has, have they? Not so far. He must wear some sort of disguise that he rips off as soon as he's done the robbery. Either that or he's someone you'd never suspect in a million years. Someone from right here in Raven Hill.'

I shivered.

Nick looked at me again. 'Lighten up, Moysten,' he murmured. 'You're getting too het up about this. Just forget about the Gripper. Ever since the cops grabbed you in Federation Park you've been acting strange. Cool it.'

I knew he was right, of course. I knew I should forget about the Gripper. But I still couldn't help thinking about the conversation afterwards. A master of disguise was scary enough. But the idea that the Gripper was someone from right here in Raven Hill, that everyone knew but no-one suspected, was even scarier.

All weekend long I couldn't keep it out of my thoughts.

17

Scary stuff

It was Monday again and Mum was trying to get Adam and Jonathon to finish their breakfasts and get ready for school. There was some drama about money for school photographs. She gave Adam the exact money but she didn't have the right change for Jonathon. So she handed him a ten-dollar note.

'Oh, Mum,' Jonathon whined. 'Ms Cafari said we have to have *exactly* the right money. She said 'specially. She said she wasn't a bank lady.'

'I don't care what Ms Cafari said,' Mum said. 'Ten dollars is all I've got. I'm not a bank lady, either.'

'Aw, Mu-um!'

'Take it or leave it.'

And there was even more drama when Jonathon saw that the ten-dollar note had a corner torn off. Someone had drawn a smiling face in ink near the tear.

'I don't want that one. It's yucky.'

'Don't be silly. Money's money.'

'Ms Cafari won't like it.'

I snatched the note away from Mum and said, 'Don't you worry, Jonathon, I'll fix it.'

I palmed the note off into the other hand and pretended to put in my mouth. Then I chewed and chewed and then swallowed and gulped. Adam and Jonathon were fascinated. You could see from their faces that they really thought I'd swallowed it.

'There,' I said. 'It's gone. No more yucky ten-dollar note.'

Brian looked up from his breakfast cereal.

'Don't teach them to put money in their mouths,' he said. 'It's filthy. You're setting a bad example.'

'I didn't really put it in my mouth,' I whispered.

'I know that,' he said. 'But they will, sure as eggs.'

The man is a moron.

'I want it! Give it back!' Jonathon squealed.

'It's all gone,' I said, taking it out of my pocket. 'But I've got another one.'

Jonathon took it and unfolded it.

'Aw, that's the same ten dollars,' he yelled. 'I can tell. It's got that face on it.'

'Oh, didn't you know?' I said. 'That's the way they're making all ten-dollar notes now.'

'Liar! Liar! Liar!' Adam shrieked, banging his spoon on his bowl in excitement. 'Do it again, Tom! Again!'

Anyway, it had worked. Jonathon agreed to take the money.

As I was going out the door, Mum said, 'Thanks, Tom. And remember we're visiting Mrs Moysten in hospital tonight.'

Mrs Moysten is my grandmother—Dad's mother. For some reason Mum always calls her Mrs Moysten when Brian's around. She seems kind of embarrassed that they're still friends even though Mum and Dad split up. Anyway, Grandma just had an eye operation and Mum thought we should both go and see her.

'Rightio,' I said.

'Make sure you finish up at the magic shop in time to meet me at six o'clock by the bank. The usual place. Brian's using the car so we'll take the bus over.'

'Sure.'

'And get some flowers from Grace's Flower Shop on the way. I'll pay you back.'

'What kind of flowers?'

'Something cheery. Tell Grace they're for your grandmother. She'll know.'

○

At school I heard the bad news about Richelle and Nick's Friday Tarquin-minding. They'd tried Elmo's talking technique and it had worked—at first. They'd walked Tarquin all around the place, talking, till their legs were nearly dropping off. And then they stopped at Richelle's house.

Richelle's sister was at home and so was her mother. How could he get into trouble with four people watching him? Well, Nick and Richelle started watching TV and everyone else was busy with something. The next thing anybody knew there were leaves all over the floor. Tarquin had picked every leaf off every pot plant in the house!

'It's winter,' he said. 'The leaves fall on the ground.'

As his mother said, he was a creative little person.

❁

When I got to the shop in the afternoon I found Sid in a jolly mood. He had his artificial arm on, and was making Jacko talk quite a bit. He seemed to have recovered from his disappointment at losing his tenants at the end of the week. I thought how stupid I'd been to let Nick's sneers about him worry me.

Sid said that he'd sold a lot of stuff over the weekend thanks to my window. He reckoned that since it was done he was getting four times as many customers as before. That's what he said.

But only a couple of people came into the shop while I was working. Was he telling the truth about all the extra customers? He must be, I thought. Why would he lie?

The storeroom was cleared out now and the rubbish had been taken away on the weekend. I pulled down some more of the magic sets that Tarquin had scrambled and spread them out on the floor. Then I started putting them back together again. It wasn't such a hard job and after about an hour I had ten complete sets ready to be taped up and sold.

Somehow the dust was really getting to me today. I kept sneezing and my eyes were watering.

'Take a break!' Sid called out. 'I don't want to get the Teen Power union on me for working you too hard.'

'I've just got a few more sets to go,' I said.

'Well, for heaven's sake, stop sneezing,' he said. 'Are you coming down with something?'

'It's the dust,' I said. 'I'll be okay in a little while.'

'Good. When you've got a minute, come here. I want to

83

cut your finger off.'

I wondered if I'd heard him right.

'The kid's got another egg in his ear, Sid,' said Jacko's voice.

'No, I heard,' I called. 'I'm on my way.'

On the counter in front of Sid, with Jacko, was a big pile of money—most of it probably the two months' rent money he'd got from the Dinkley's. But there was also a small metal gadget. I'd never seen anything like it before.

'What's that?' I asked.

'You know those things that cut the ends off expensive cigars? The things with a razor blade in them and you put the cigar in and *bam*! you hit it with your fist and it slices the end of the cigar off?'

I'd never heard of anything like that.

'Not really,' I said.

'The boy doesn't smoke cigars, Sid,' said Jacko.

'I didn't imagine he did, Jacko,' said Sid.

'So what's the point, Sid?'

'I'm explaining this gizmo to him, Jacko. It's like a cigar cutter. Here, Tom, put your finger in.'

I stuck out my finger and brought it close to the hole.

'Watch it,' warned Jacko. 'That thing's sharp!'

What am I doing? I thought. This guy is about to cut my finger off and I'm letting him do it!

Sid grabbed my hand gently in his and pushed my finger into the hole as far as it would go.

'There now,' he said, raising his fist in the air to hit the lever. 'Off it comes!'

Suddenly he stopped.

'No,' he said, pulling out a carrot from under the counter, 'maybe we'd better try it out on this first, just to make sure it's working.'

I pulled out my finger and he put the carrot in. Then he pounded the top of the cutter with his fist and the carrot fell into two neat pieces.

'Works all right, Sid,' said Jacko.

'Yup,' said Sid. 'It works on carrots, anyway. Now let's give it the finger test.'

I hesitated.

'What's wrong, Tom?' he asked.

'I—I don't know,' I said.

'He's scared to death, if you ask me, Sid,' said Jacko. 'Doesn't trust you.'

'Don't you trust old Sigmund the Sorcerer, Tom? I thought you were the sorcerer's apprentice!'

'Well—'

'I wouldn't trust him either,' said Jacko.

Slowly I put my finger into the cutting hole. In a flash, Sid's artificial hand had grabbed my wrist, jamming the finger in place. He raised his fist in the air again.

'No!' I yelled, screwing my eyes shut.

Sid's fist pounded the top of the cutter with a crash. In that terrifying moment I could feel the cold steel of the blade and I knew that my finger was lying in a pool of blood on the counter.

I opened my eyes to see Sid's face. For a minute I didn't move. I was still sure my finger had been sliced in two. Then I pulled it slowly out of the cutter.

My finger was okay. There was only a slight red line

across the top where the metal had touched it.

'Bad luck, Sid,' said Jacko.

'I guess I'd better get the blade sharpened,' Sid laughed. 'That thing wouldn't slice anything but carrots. Hey, are you all right?'

I don't know if it was the sneezing or the fear but I rocked back on my heels and felt like I was going to faint.

'I'm okay,' I said.

'It's just a trick,' Sid said. 'If I'd have known it was going to affect you that way—'

'I'm okay,' I said again.

'Tom, you've been working too hard. You're jumpy as a cat. I want you to take a day off, all right? I don't want you to come in tomorrow. You need more time to relax and to get some studying done. I'll pay you just the same—'

'No way.'

'I owe it to you for all your good suggestions. You've made a lot of money for me.'

I knew I'd had no reason to be scared, but that finger-cutting business had kind of given me the creeps. Besides, Sid was just the last in a long line of people to say I was being jumpy and strange lately. I found I quite liked the idea of having a day off.

'All right. Thanks,' I said.

'And would you mind closing up tonight? I've left my car at the service station and I have to go over to pick it up before it closes.'

I looked at the stack of money on the counter.

'Are you going to leave all that money here?' I asked.

'I'll put it in the till. It'll be okay. No-one ever breaks in here. I'm just too busy to put it in the bank.'

'I'll bank it for you on my way home,' I said. 'You just fill out one of those slips and put it in an envelope.'

'You're a treasure, Tom.'

Sid put the money in an envelope, dropped it in the till and then left the shop.

I stayed on, pleased that I'd be able to help. Without any idea of what was to come.

18

The attack

Wouldn't you know, just when I was going to close the shop, these kids came in with their mother and they wanted to play with everything.

It was getting close to six and I was trying to hurry them out, but they just kept looking at things. I didn't want to be rude, of course. They were Sid's customers, not mine.

Finally they bought two jigsaw puzzles and an expensive magic set. It was a great sale. I couldn't wait to tell Sid about it.

At five to six I put the envelope from the till in my schoolbag, locked the door and sprinted down the street to where I was supposed to meet Mum.

Needless to say, I was late. And Mum wasn't impressed.

'Sorry,' I panted. 'I was closing up and there was a customer.'

'Where are the flowers?'

The flowers! I'd completely forgotten the flowers!

'I'll get them now,' I said.

'Grace has probably closed by now. She closes at six and it's already ten past.'

88

'I'll see,' I said, throwing my bag down at her feet. 'Keep an eye on that. I'll be right back.'

I raced off around the corner and up a couple blocks. The flower shop was dark, but Grace was outside hosing down the footpath.

'I need some flowers,' I begged. 'It's urgent!'

Grace laughed.

'I haven't got much left,' she warned. But she opened the door of the shop and let me go in. I grabbed a bunch of little pink rosebuds, plonked down the money and was out the door shouting my thanks in a minute.

It was when I was running back along the dark street with the flowers in my hand that I sensed that something was wrong. I don't know why, but I just had this feeling. Then I came around the corner and Mum was nowhere in sight. My heart skipped a beat.

I peered around in the darkness. Then I saw her—lying on the ground by the wall.

'Mum!'

I heard her groan before I reached her.

'Mum!'

'I'm all right,' she croaked. She began struggling to get up, holding her hand to her throat.

'Was it . . .? Did you . . .?' I stammered, trying to help her.

'The phone—over there . . . Quickly! Dial triple O . . .'

Sure enough, it had been the Gripper. The police were there in a flash, but it didn't do much good. As usual, the Gripper had got clean away. Nobody nearby had seen anyone running or anyone acting suspiciously.

While Mum was talking to the police, her right eye

became more and more swollen until it was completely closed.

'We'll take you to hospital,' one of the police officers said.

'No! No, thank you,' Mum whispered, holding on to my hand. 'It's okay, really. I just want to get home and cancel my credit cards.'

'The Gripper doesn't use stolen credit cards. If he did we'd 've caught him by now,' the officer said. 'It's up to you, ma'am, but I'd get the eye seen to. Now, could you just briefly go over what you told us one last time?'

'As I said, I was waiting here for Tom,' Mum began wearily. 'He's been working in the afternoons at Sid's Magic Shop. He arrived, and then ran back to buy some flowers for his grandmother.'

I stood by helplessly, listening. If only I hadn't forgotten the flowers! If only I hadn't left Mum alone like that. If only . . .

'I didn't hear the Gripper coming up behind me,' Mum said. 'I didn't hear a thing. The first I knew was when his arm went around my throat. He was strong. Really strong. He sort of jerked my head back so I nearly choked. And there was this thing poking in my back. A gun, maybe.'

I felt her hand tighten on mine.

'He grabbed my bag,' she went on. 'He told me not to move or look at him and to count to fifty. Just when he let go, I turned my head sideways for a second. I didn't mean to. It was just automatic. That's when he hit me and I fell down.'

'So you must have seen him when you turned,' the police officer said.

'Not properly.' Mum shuddered. 'I got just a glimpse before he hit me and—it was horrible!'

'Horrible? In what way?'

'I can't describe it.' Mum shuddered again. 'He was dead pale, and snarling at me. And he'd been—hurt.' She paused.

'Hurt?' urged the officer.

'I think he had a deep cut on his forehead running down over his eye, and some other scars, too,' Mum said. 'It was just horrible. Nightmarish.' She stopped again, and swallowed. 'Sorry,' she said, 'I'm being silly. It can't have been as bad as that.'

'Shock can play tricks on our memories,' said the officer, closing his notebook. 'Don't worry about it any more now, ma'am. We'll call on you again in the morning, when you've had a chance to calm down.'

The police offered to give us a lift home. It was only then that I looked around for my schoolbag.

'Hey! Where's my bag?' I yelled.

'He must have taken it,' Mum said helplessly. 'I didn't notice.'

'Oh, no!' I cried. 'It had a whole lot of Sid's money in it. I was going to deposit it at the Autobank for him.'

My stomach knotted up. I couldn't believe it! I looked around again, desperately, but the bag was gone.

'How much money?' the policeman asked. 'Not so much, surely. Old Sid doesn't exactly make a fortune out of that shop, by the look of it.'

'I don't know exactly what was there,' I said. 'But there was an awful lot. A whole wad of it. Oh no! What am I going to do? I'll have to tell him!'

'You go home with your mother,' said the police officer. 'Sid lives at the caravan park these days, doesn't he? He's a harmless old bloke, but we keep an eye on him all the same, if you know what I mean. We'll go out there and see him. We'll tell him. Just leave it to us.'

I was glad to. I didn't want to see Sid's face when he found out what had happened. His profits *and* his rent money—gone with the Gripper. And all because of me!

19

The face

Brian was really upset, of course. He wanted Mum to go to hospital too, but she wouldn't hear of it. She phoned Grandma to say that we weren't coming to visit because she wasn't feeling well. She didn't tell the whole story so as not to worry her.

Jonathon listened to everything and then told us proudly about his own *personal* robbery.

'I didn't get my school photos,' he said brightly.

Of course nobody was particularly interested what with Brian checking out Mum's black eye and me worrying about Sid.

'Guess what happened?' Jonathon asked. 'Guess why I didn't get my photos?'

'The camera broke when they took a picture of you,' I said.

'No,' he said. 'Tarquin stole the money.'

'What?! Why that little—!'

'He took the envelope out of my bag.'

'Did you see him do it?'

'No. But he did it,' Jonathon said firmly. 'He always steals stuff.'

'Did you tell your teacher?' Brian asked Jonathon.

'Yes.'

'And what did she say.'

'She said nobody saw Tarquin take the money. So she said maybe someone else tooked it.'

While all this was going on I had a bright idea.

'Mum,' I said, 'you know those police artists' drawings? The ones they draw from witnesses' descriptions? To help identify criminals?'

'What about them?'

'You tell me what the Gripper looked like and I'll draw a picture!'

'I don't think I'm remembering him properly, Tom,' Mum said. 'I was so scared and shocked. There was only a glance. And what I thought I saw was so—weird.'

'I know, you said that,' I said. 'But let's give it a go, okay?'

I'll say this for Mum: even though she was still shaken up from the robbery, she was a good sport. I did sketch after sketch of the Gripper's face just from her saying things like, 'No, the nose was flatter' and 'The scar is longer and closer to his eyebrows.'

It was the most hideous face I'd ever seen. We were all sure that if he lived in Raven Hill we'd have noticed him, and remembered.

And yet, I did remember the face. I'd seen it before, maybe a long time ago. Or was it a face from a TV program or a magazine? Somewhere the face had crept quietly into my memory. And now I knew it wouldn't go away until the mystery of the Gripper was solved.

●

All I could think about that night was the police breaking the news to Sid. This would certainly put him out of business. I felt so guilty. If only I'd let him leave the money in the shop it would still be safe.

At school the next day I was a major celebrity. Everybody wanted to know about the robbery. I told the Teen Power gang but then I got tired of going over the same old story to everyone else. And I didn't tell anyone about Sid's money.

I thought of ringing him but I couldn't bring myself to do it. I wouldn't have to see him that afternoon but, sooner or later, I was going to have to face the music.

Liz caught up to me in the corridor.

'Big problems,' she said. 'Nick and Richelle say they won't look after Tarquin again.'

'You can hardly blame them, can you?'

'I know, but his parents are out till five-thirty. I can't contact them.'

'So?'

'So someone's got to pick him up from school.'

'Can't Nick and Richelle just take him straight to his house and stay there with him?'

'Tom, you don't understand: Richelle wants to kill him— and so does Nick. They've absolutely refused. They say they'll quit Teen Power Inc. rather than deal with him.'

'How about Sunny and Elmo?' I said. 'They're the only ones who can handle the kid.'

'Elmo and I had him yesterday and he was okay. We spent

two hours talking to him. You just can't ignore him, that's all. You have to be prepared to spend two hours talking to him and playing with him.'

'Well then you can do it again today,' I said. 'Simple.'

'It's Tuesday. Elmo's busy helping his father at the *Pen*, I have to meet my mum at four-thirty to go shopping. Sunny's supposed to be walking the dog today. That's only an hour so I can do that instead of her and she can take Tarquin. But she can't do it alone.'

She paused. I waited. I knew what was coming.

'Nick said you're not working at the shop today,' she said casually, at last.

'Oh, no you don't, Liz!' I said. 'I never wanted to look after the kid in the first place! I warned you.'

'It's good money.'

'I don't care how much it is. Do you realise that little monster stole ten dollars from my brother?'

'Sunny knows how to handle him, believe me,' Liz said. She began backing away. 'Just meet her at Raven Hill Primary at three-thirty,' she gabbled. 'Bye!' She started running while I still had my mouth open to protest. 'Thanks, Tom, you're a prince,' she called back over her shoulder.

'Make that a pushover,' I grumbled to myself. 'OK, I'll do it. But I won't like it.'

Sunny and I picked Tarquin up from school and walked him back to his flat. Mrs Anderson had left the key under a pot plant so we could let ourselves in.

From Tarquin's place I could see the back of the row of shops where Sid's place was. Next door to him was an empty building with a broken-down old garage behind it. Vines were growing all over the garage doors. The place was dark, abandoned for years after the shop had gone out of business. I wondered if Sid's would be the same some day.

For the moment the new bright lights were on in the magic shop, lighting the lane behind.

'That's the crazy man,' Tarquin said, pointing at the shop. 'He's crazy!'

I kept thinking about going over and talking to Sid. Maybe I should go over that evening after minding the little monster. I couldn't leave it till the next day. Chances were Sid wouldn't want to see me ever again anyway. Who could blame him?

Sunny had this really good way with Tarquin. She'd talk to him right on his level like she was his age. I was hopeless. I'd think of a question like, 'What do you want to be when you grow up,' and he'd say, 'I don't know. That's stupid!' I guess I just didn't have the knack.

Then I had a better idea. I pulled out a handkerchief and poked it down into my fist the way Sid had taught me. Then I blew on it and opened my hand and it was gone.

'How did you do that?!' Tarquin squealed.

'Magic, my boy, magic.'

'How? How? How?'

He loved it. I did it again and again.

Then I pulled a twenty-cent piece out of his ear and he loved that one too. And I made it disappear.

'I'll show you how to do it,' I said, and I did it in slow

motion, showing him how I pretended to put it in one hand but really put it in the other.

'You're not bad,' Sunny said. 'I'm impressed.'

'Years of practice,' I said.

That's when Tarquin decided to do it himself. I told him to use his own coin. (Why should I let the kid rip me off?) He searched his pockets and came up with a ten-dollar note. Not just any ten-dollar note, though. It was Jonathon's ten-dollar note!

'Hey!' I said, grabbing it out of his hand. 'Where did you get that?'

Tarquin got really angry and tried to grab it back.

'What are you doing?' Sunny said in surprise.

'Look at this,' I said, showing her the note. 'See that torn corner and the face? I've seen this note before. I happen to know who it belongs to.' I rounded on Tarquin. 'Don't you *ever* take someone else's money again,' I said to him.

He looked very embarrassed, and didn't say anything when I put the note in my pocket.

20

Facing the music

I thought of telling Tarquin's parents about the ten dollars, but in the end I didn't. I'd got it back, after all. Why complicate things? It was bad enough that they were up for the price of seven tropical fish and about fifteen pot plants.

I told Sunny about Sid's lost money and she called in at the magic shop with me. I told her she didn't have to, but I was really glad she did.

Sid was there, getting ready to close the shop.

'Is your mother all right?' he said, as soon as he saw me.

So the police *had* spoken to him, like they said they would.

'She's just kind of shaken, that's all,' I said. 'She's got a black eye.'

He shook his head. 'I couldn't believe it when the cops told me,' he said. 'Your mother!' He shook his head again. 'It's a terrible thing, all these robberies. It's not safe to walk the streets anymore.'

'Sid—?' I began.

'Yes, Tom?'

'You know that money I was going to bank last night?'

'The police told me,' he said. 'The Gripper got it. Never

mind. It wasn't your fault.'

He was so calm! I couldn't believe it.

'I'll pay you back,' I mumbled, feeling my cheeks get hot.

'Moneybags!' squarked Jacko, from a shadowy corner.

Sid grinned. 'How could you do that? Be sensible, Tom. Let's just chalk it up to experience.'

'Well I don't have the money now,' I said, 'but I'll earn it. I'll pay it off bit by bit. I promise.'

Sid laughed aloud this time.

'That's very kind of you,' he said, 'but I couldn't expect you to do that. No, it was my decision to let you take the money. I was responsible for what happened.'

'But Sid—'

'No arguments, Tom. This is your day off, so let's not discuss it any more. Off you go. I'll see you tomorrow.'

'You're crazy, Sid!' said Jacko.

'That'll be enough, Jacko!'

'Sorry, Sid!'

○

Sunny and I stopped at a cafe up the street and I bought a couple of milkshakes with the torn ten-dollar note. I could pay Mum back later.

We sat at a table outside, on the footpath, drinking the milkshakes, and then I saw Donelle and Dave walking towards us, arm in arm. Donelle saw me, and said something to Dave. She seemed to be trying to persuade him to do something, because at first he shook his head, and then shrugged his shoulders. I wondered what was up.

They stopped at our table. 'Not working at the shop today, mate?' said Dave in a casual sort of way. 'Job finished, is it?'

'No,' I said. 'I'm just having the afternoon off.'

I thought they looked disappointed. 'Why?' I said. 'Is there a problem?'

They both shook their heads violently. 'Oh, no! No!' said Dave, looking embarrassed. 'We were just—you know, wondering.'

Donelle nudged him.

He glanced at Sunny and then back at me. 'We just thought—you know—that shop doesn't seem—you know— the best sort of place for a kid to be spending all that time,' he blundered on. 'That's all we thought.'

'It's okay,' I said coldly. Why was everyone against me? I fumed. Why was everyone always trying to stop me doing things I wanted to do?

'Oh. Right.' Dave glanced at Donelle. 'Well, we'd better be off,' he said. 'Give the old girl her exercise.'

'Dave!' smiled Donelle. 'You're awful!'

They waved and went on, moving carefully past the tables so Donelle's big stomach wouldn't bash into anything.

'It's good she likes to exercise,' Sunny said. 'Mum says too many women get out of shape when they're going to have a baby. They seem quite nice.'

'They're boring. But still, I wish they weren't leaving the flat,' I said. 'Sid really needs that money, I know he does.'

'Do you feel better now that you've talked to him?'

'I guess so,' I said. 'I still feel really bad, though. He was so *nice* about it.'

Sunny slurped the last of her milkshake.

'It was a bit weird, wasn't it?' she said.

'What was?'

'Just what you said. He's taken losing the money so well. Nobody loses that much money and stays calm about it. The average person would go off their brain.'

'Sid's not your average person,' I said.

'That's for sure,' said Sunny. And looked thoughtfully at me.

In my dreams that night I was walking alone through an old warehouse. There was water dripping onto the floor from above. Where was it coming from? I found an old staircase and went up. There in the middle of a huge empty room was a plastic bucket like the one I'd been using to clean the magic shop. I came up to it slowly and looked inside. There, in a pool of blood, was the Gripper's face looking up at me.

That face! I let out an ear-piercing scream.

'Are you all right, darling?'

It was Mum, sitting on the edge of my bed, running her fingers through my sweaty hair.

'I'm okay,' I mumbled. 'Just a bad dream.'

'It's the Gripper, isn't it?' she said. She shivered. 'I've been having nightmares myself. But, really, we should try to forget him, darling.'

'I'm all right, Mum. Don't worry.'

'Tom?'

'Yes?'

'From now on could you leave the magic shop in

plenty of time to get home before dark?'

'Sure.'

○

When I got to the shop on Wednesday Sid was in an even better mood than he'd been the night before. But there was something really strange about him—like he was really excited about something, something he didn't want to tell me about. I hadn't ever seen him like this. And Jacko was jokier than ever.

'There'll be some more cleaning work when Dave and Donelle leave next Saturday, Tom,' he said. 'Got to get the flat ready for a new tenant—namely me.'

'And me, Sid,' said Jacko.

'Of course, Jacko. I do apologise.'

'Aren't you even going to *try* to find someone to rent it?' I said.

'Oh, no. I'm looking forward to moving in again. Now the shop's on its feet I want to be right where the action is. I want to keep an eye on things. Especially with the new plan in operation.'

Sid looked at me with a twinkle in his eye.

'What plan?' I asked.

'*Your* plan, Tom,' he said. 'How soon you forget! The computer games and all that other mumbo-jumbo stuff.'

'Are you serious?'

'No! He's crazy!' Jacko piped up.

'Take no notice of him,' Sid said. 'Have a look in the storeroom.'

Sure enough, there in the back were cartons and cartons

of new games, books—and even a computer!

'Of course you'll have to help me get set up,' Sid said. 'I'm relying on you.'

I couldn't believe my eyes.

'How did you do this?,' I asked.

'You mean where did I get the money?'

'Well, yes.'

'If I told you that Sigmund the Sorcerer just made it appear out of thin air, would you believe me?' Sid laughed. 'Or don't you really believe in magic?'

'Well, not when it comes to money,' I said.

'The kid's not as silly as he looks, Sid,' said Jacko.

'That'll be enough, Jacko.'

'Sorry, Sid.'

'Come on, then,' Sid grinned at me. 'What are you waiting for? There's a computer to set up and lots of stock to put out on the shelves. There's an old dog here who wants to learn some new tricks! Hop to! Rally round!'

It was like a dream come true. In an hour we had a whole aisle stocked with the new games and I'd even managed to set up the computer and show Sid how to run a demo of one of the games: 'Revenge of the Cyber Punks'.

A few customers came in, bought things and left again. One of them even bought a computer game. The next time the door screamed and laughed, it was Mum. She'd brought Adam and Jonathon along with her.

Jonathon's eyes lit up when he saw the computer and he started playing with it straightaway.

'I'm Grace Murphy, Tom's mother,' Mum said to Sid. 'I just thought I'd see how things were going.'

104

'I was sorry to hear about your . . . your accident,' Sid said, looking at Mum's black eye.

'I'll be okay in a few days. It's the shock of the thing,' Mum said. 'I'm sorry you had to lose *your* money.'

'Don't be, dear lady. It was just one of those things. You win a few and you lose a few.'

'You lost an arm,' said Jacko. 'When are you going to win one, Sid?'

Adam and Jonathon stared at him, open-mouthed.

'That'll be enough, Jacko!'

'Sorry, Sid.'

Mum smiled. 'Tom,' she said, turning to me, 'have you shown Mr Foy the sketch you made of the Gripper?'

Sid jumped. 'You actually *saw* him?' he asked me.

'Mum did,' I said. 'I just sketched him from Mum's description. It really doesn't look like anything.'

I took the drawing out of my bag and showed it to Sid. Maybe I imagined it, but he looked shocked. He turned to me.

'If I were you,' he said, 'I'd keep that hidden. Don't show it around.'

'Do you know who it is?'

'No, I don't. But it's pretty obvious that this guy doesn't want anyone to see him. He may not know you saw him, Mrs Murphy. I wouldn't show it around if I were you. Have the police seen it?'

'No,' I said.

'Good. My advice would be to keep it to yourself. The fewer people who know about it, the better.'

21

A secret place

'Pete had his money stolen at school,' Jonathon said.

'Pete who?' I asked.

'Pete Free.'

Liz's little brother. That miniature crook Tarquin had come out of retirement already!

'Luckily Jonathon lent Pete some money for lunch,' Mum said. 'Right, Jonno?'

'I found a two dollars in my bag,' Jonathon said proudly. 'I think it was left over from the photos money.'

'What are you talking about?' I asked.

'The photos money envelope must have tore,' he said. 'Some money fell out. So Tarquin didn't get it all. Sucks!'

'Now, wait a minute. What's this about two dollars? You didn't have any coins. You had a ten-dollar note,' I said, remembering the money I'd taken back from Tarquin.

'No, he didn't,' Mum said.

'But I saw it,' I said. 'A ten-dollar note. It was torn. It had a little face on it.'

'No,' Mum said. 'I took that one back. Brian found the right money for Jonathon to take in the end.'

'What happened to the ten-dollar note?'

'I put it back in my bag. I guess the Gripper got it.'

The Gripper? If the Gripper got it, how had Tarquin ended up with it? Tarquin might be a real pain, but he couldn't possibly be the Gripper!

'Listen, Tom,' Mum said, 'I've got to get back and start dinner. Do you want me to send Brian down to pick you up?'

'No, thanks anyway. I'll get back before dark.'

'Promise?'

'Promise.'

○

Sid let me go about fifteen minutes early. But I had to know where Tarquin had got that ten-dollar note, so I ducked around to the back to wait for Liz and Sunny to bring Tarquin home.

I watched Donelle and Dave come down the back stairs at Sid's and out into the lane, starting off on their evening walk.

They noticed me and stared. I suppose I must have looked odd, hanging around like that. But then Dave grinned and Donelle gave me a friendly wave. I waved back and they walked on, with Donelle clinging to Dave's arm. I wondered if he really would be a match for the Gripper. He was strong, but he wasn't too bright. And Donelle certainly wouldn't be. Not in her condition. I hoped Sid was right when he said they'd be safe.

○

The wait was longer than I expected. The sun had disappeared behind the block of flats and I knew Mum would be worrying about me by now.

Finally, Sunny and Tarquin came along. Liz wasn't with them.

'She had to go home,' Sunny explained, 'so I brought him back on my own. He's actually being a good kid, aren't you Tarquin?'

'Yup,' said Tarquin.

'Tarquin,' I said, kneeling down to be on his level, 'I have a very important question to ask you.'

The kid looked at me very suspiciously.

'Remember the ten dollars I took from you?' I said. 'I'd like you to tell me where you got it.'

'What is this about?' Sunny asked. 'Didn't he get it at school?'

'I don't think so,' I said. 'Tell me, Tarks.'

Tarquin shook his head from side to side.

'Please,' I pleaded.

Tarquin just shook his head again.

'I'll tell you what,' I said, getting a box out of my pocket. 'This is itching power. Put it down someone's shirt and they'll itch like crazy. Think of all the fun you can have with it.'

He grabbed for it and I pulled it back, out of reach.

'Not so fast,' I said. 'You tell me where you got the ten dollars and then I'll give it to you.'

'Promise?'

'Cross my heart and hope to die. How about it?'

'Over there,' Tarquin said, pointing across the lane.

He led us to the old garage beside the backyard of the

magic shop. He pulled the weeds and ivy aside and wiggled through a small space between the double doors.

'Hey! Where'd you go? Come out of there!' I whispered.

Sunny and I squeezed through the gap and into the garage. It was getting dark now and it was even darker inside. Only the light from Sid's shop next door, streaming through the cracks in the boards, showed us the piles of old broken furniture and other things stacked around the walls.

In the corner Tarquin was kneeling over a black plastic bag. He opened the top so that we could see inside.

'Tom!' Sunny exclaimed. 'It's full of handbags and wallets!'

We started looking through the bag. There were dozens of bags and wallets there. Everything was still in them—drivers' licences, credit cards, all sorts of junk. Everything but the money. On top was my schoolbag and Mum's handbag. Sure enough, Mum's money was missing and so was Sid's rent money.

Sunny and I looked at each other.

'It's the Gripper's stuff, isn't it?' Sunny said.

'You're not wrong,' I answered. 'Was the ten dollars in here?' I asked Tarquin.

'Over there,' he said, pointing to the ground.

'He must have dropped it,' Sunny said. 'Or maybe he didn't want it because it was marked. Maybe he thought he'd be caught if he tried to spend it.'

I stood there looking at it for a minute, thinking. Trying to piece things together.

Who was he, this man with the horrible face? He must live nearby. The shop next to Sid's was abandoned, but what if the Gripper had been camping in there? No-one would know. And this garage would be a perfect dumping ground for the evidence of his robberies. No-one would ever look in here. No-one except a nosy, naughty little kid.

I went to look at the door that led into the abandoned shop's backyard. It was bolted shut. And the bolt was rusty and covered in spider webs.

'Let's get out of here!' Sunny whispered. 'Call the police!'

'Just a minute. There's something I can't understand.'

'What?'

'The Gripper must be very skinny to get into this place. Those doors, front and back, haven't been opened in years. And I only just made it through that gap that leads out to the lane. If the Gripper's been squeezing through that over and over again the ivy would be all smashed up, surely.'

Tarquin stood up and pointed to the side wall. There was a sheet of plywood propped up against it. I grabbed it and slid it sideways along the ground. There in the wall behind was a big hole—big enough for anyone to climb through. Light streamed through it from the back of the magic shop.

'That's it!' Sunny whispered. 'That's how he gets in! First he gets into Sid's backyard and then he just climbs through.'

Suddenly it struck me like a thunderbolt. The face! The Gripper's face! No wonder Mum had called it nightmarish and horrible! It was one of those rubber masks from the magic shop.

My mind was in a whirl. The Gripper! Someone everyone knew but no-one would suspect in a million years, Nick had said. Someone who needed money, and didn't know how else to get it, Brian had said.

The pieces fell into place like a horrible jigsaw. The Gripper. Someone who could disguise his voice. Someone who could disappear like magic. Someone with one strong arm to catch his victims around the throat, and something hard to press against their backs. Like a gun—or metal hand . . .

I made a choking sound.

Outside, something moved.

'What was that?' Sunny whispered.

Then suddenly there he was, crouching by the hole looking in, blocking out the light.

'Sid!' I yelled. 'Sid!'

He grabbed the piece of plywood in his hand and threw it to the side, his body now halfway through the hole.

Tarquin screamed and we ran for the doors but a powerful arm shot out, punching me in the back of the head. A white flash of pain shot through my skull as I went crashing over a barrel and into a pile of flowerpots, sending them flying in all directions.

'Run, Sunny! Tarquin! Get the cops!' I screamed.

But Sunny was spinning around. Then she was leaping, twisting, her feet crashing into the man's stomach. He grunted, doubled over. And Sunny's leg was flashing forward, hitting him squarely under the chin and sending him crashing to the ground.

It was only when he lay there, unconscious on the ground, that we saw who it really was.

Dave. I couldn't believe my eyes. Stupid, macho Dave Dinkley was the Gripper!

'Let's get out of here!' I screamed, crawling over to Sunny and struggling to my feet.

111

'No, you don't!'

A hard arm grabbed me around the throat as the new voice growled the words.

Even as I struggled against the strangling grip, and heard Sunny's gasping cries as she too fought our attacker, my mind registered the shock.

Donelle!

Her arms were like iron bands. She had us both, one on each side, and we gasped for breath as she squeezed tighter and tighter. I tried kicking at her legs but it was no use. In terror I felt myself drifting into unconsciousness.

'Help!' I tried to scream, but nothing more than a soft croak came out.

Suddenly Donelle gave a huff of surprise. Then she swore. Her strangling grip around our necks loosened. And the next moment she was writhing on the ground with Tarquin standing over her, emptying the last of the box of itching powder all over her body.

'I'll get you for this!' Donelle screamed, frantically tearing at her clothes and rubbing at her legs and arms and neck. 'You . . .!'

Sunny was on her feet in a second, grabbing ropes and rags from the garage floor, looping them around the struggling Donelle's feet and hands, and pulling them tight.

I tried to do the same thing with Dave. He was stirring. My hands were shaking as I fumbled with the knots. The ropes and rag were old. How long would they hold? I thought. Long enough for us to get away? For us to get through the gap in the door, across the dark lane, disappear into Tarquin's flat where they couldn't find us? Long enough for . . .?

'Hey! Look at this!' Sunny gasped.

There in the half-light we saw it. On Donelle's stomach, where her smock had bunched up as she writhed and struggled. It was hard and round, like a bowl or the shell of a big turtle, strapped around the woman's body. Sunny grabbed it and pulled it away and when she did, a handbag, a toy gun and a hideous rubber mask fell out.

'She's not pregnant at all!' Sunny yelled. 'She just used her false stomach to carry the loot. No wonder the Gripper always got away so fast! Who'd suspect a pregnant woman and her husband? And even if they did, the stolen stuff was completely hidden.'

Donelle was baring her teeth at us, growling with rage, pulling at the ropes that bound her.

'You'll be sorry,' she spat at me. 'I thought you were up to something, hanging round in the lane. I knew you'd be trouble, poking around. When I catch you . . .'

She was getting loose! I grabbed Sunny's hand and Tarquin's shirt and started hurrying them towards the gap in the door.

But Dave had got to his knees now. He was ripping and tearing with his teeth at the rags on his wrists. In one minute . . . half a minute . . .

'This is the police! Don't anybody in there move! Stay right where you are!' barked a voice from the magic shop backyard.

'In there, Franco! Cover me!' shouted another voice from the lane.

Sirens filled the air.

The police! I was never so relieved in all my life!

The police went on barking orders and shouting to each other. There must be six of them out there at least, I figured. More than enough to beat Dave and Donelle.

'Lie flat on the floor, face down, you two. Send the children out!' the first voice ordered. 'One at a time. And no funny business or we'll come in firing!'

At that, Donelle and Dave stopped struggling and lay back. They knew when they were beaten.

Shaking like a leaf I crawled after Tarquin into the magic shop backyard. Sunny came after me.

We stood up and looked around for the police team.

And saw an empty yard full of voices—and Sid!

22

Teen Power strikes again!

The police did arrive soon after that, of course. They got into the garage, handcuffed the Dinkleys and took them away. I sometimes wonder if Donelle and Dave ever worked out that the voices and sirens that had made them give up hadn't been the police at all. That all of them had been Sid. He really is a great ventriloquist. And he'd just given the performance of his life.

They'd have been so angry if they knew. The police had come as quickly as they could, once Sid called them. But the Dinkleys could easily have got to us—and got away clean—before they arrived, if Sid hadn't taken matters into his own hands. Or hand, as Jacko put it.

The police had called Mum, Sunny's mother and Tarquin's parents. They all arrived in a panicking bunch just as the police van left.

Sid was the hero of the day. He stood in the magic shop with Jacko on his good arm, surrounded by his fans.

'We can't thank you enough,' Mum told Sid, 'for rescuing

Tom. How did you know he was in the garage?'

'I heard him,' said Sid simply. 'I was hanging around in the shop, see. I was sort of keeping an eye out for Dave and Donelle, waiting for them to get back from their walk. Just after they came in the back gate, I heard Tom yell my name. That was enough for me. I rang the cops. Then I went out for Tom.'

He grinned at Sunny and Tarquin. 'He didn't really need me, of course, from what I hear. He had tae-kwon-do Tilly and Tarquin the Terrible to protect him.'

Sunny's mother laughed and Sunny looked embarrassed, but Tarquin pushed out his chest and his parents beamed with pride. I groaned to myself. There'd be no holding the kid now.

'Sid,' I accused, 'you mean you knew all the time that Dave and Donelle were doing the Gripper robberies?' I said.

'Oh, no. I didn't start suspecting them till yesterday. The sketch you showed me tipped me off. I knew that face was one of my old masks. Dave and Donelle could have taken it from the storeroom at any time when they came in through the back door of the shop.'

'But anyone could have bought one of those masks,' Sunny said.

'I guess they could,' Sid shrugged. 'But not lately. They were old stock. I haven't sold one in years. I was afraid you'd show the sketch to the police, Tom and they'd suspect *me*,' he added with a laugh. 'Can you imagine that: *me*, Jack the Gripper?'

'No, not really,' I said, smiling uncomfortably. I knew I could never tell him that for a few mad moments I actually *had* imagined it. Very clearly.

'But anyway, it wasn't just the mask, the mask just started me thinking. About the Dinkleys. How harmless and respectable they looked. How they went for that walk every night. How the Gripper attacks had started around the time they took the flat.'

He grinned. 'And then there was Donelle herself, and her smocks, and the so-called baby on the way. I thought about how in all the time she'd been here, she didn't seem to get any bigger. When they took the flat four months ago, she looked like she was ready to have a baby any minute. When she said the baby wasn't due for a few more months I thought, "Hang on, is she having a baby or an elephant?" But I put it out of my mind till last night.'

'At the end of this week they'd have been off and away,' I said. 'Lucky we caught them when we did.'

'Otherwise for sure they'd be lying low for a while then starting up business somewhere else,' Sunny's mother put in.

'At least their business pays, Sid,' said Jacko. 'Unlike some.'

'Crime doesn't pay, Jacko,' said Sid sternly.

'Oh, yes. I forgot. Sorry, Sid.'

The good news is that very soon after that Sid's Magic and Games became the hottest business in Raven Hill. Kids came from everywhere to buy games and to see Sid in his magician's outfit and to listen to Jacko's corny jokes.

Elmo's dad wrote a front-page article for the *Pen* about Sid, with a headline that said SID'S MAGIC GRIPS THE

GRIPPER and in no time his face was in newspapers and magazines all over Australia and even on TV.

Money and fame didn't change him, though. He went on just as before. Like I said to Sunny, Sid really isn't your average person.

But there were two more mysteries to be solved: Who stole Jonathon's photo money? Well, I'm sorry, but nobody knows that to this day. And, as for the mysterious 'magic' money that helped Sid finance his shop's new look? Simple, a loan from the bank. And now that's all paid off.

Teen Power Inc. got lots of credit of course, and that was great for business. But one person who deserves special mention is Tarquin. When it came to itching powder, that kid really was creative after all.

Emily Rodda's

Raven Hill Mysteries 1

THE GHOST OF RAVEN HILL

Mystery and adventure are the last things Liz has in mind when she forms Teen Power Inc. All she and her friends want to do is earn some money.

But an ordinary paper round job turns into a nightmare for the gang. Not everyone in Raven Hill wants the *Pen* newspaper delivered. *Somebody* will stop at nothing – however vicious – to see the paper fold!

Emily Rodda's

Raven Hill Mysteries 3

THE DISAPPEARING TV STAR

Fame is round the corner for Richelle – or so she thinks.
At last, Liz has found the gang a job worth doing –
extras in a TV ad. But Richelle's big break turns into
a nightmare when the star of the ad disappears. Now
Richelle is on the terrifying trail of kidnappers!

Raven Hill Mysteries
Emily Rodda

629924	The Ghost of Raven Hill	£2.99	❏
629932	The Sorcerer's Apprentice	£2.99	❏
629940	The Disappearing TV Star	£2.99	❏
629959	Cry of the Cat	£2.99	❏
629967	Beware the Gingerbread House (August 95)	£2.99	❏
629975	Green for Danger (August 95)	£2.99	❏

All Hodder Children's books are available at your local bookshop or newsagent, or can be ordered direct from the publisher. Just tick the titles you want and fill in the form below. Prices and availability subject to change without notice.

Hodder Children's Books, Cash Sales Department, Bookpoint, 39 Milton Park, Abingdon, OXON, OX14 4TD, UK. If you have a credit card you may order by telephone – 0235 831700.

Please enclose a cheque or postal order made payable to Bookpoint Ltd to the value of the cover price and allow the following for postage and packing:
UK & BFPO – £1.00 for the first book, 50p for the second book, and 30p for each additional book ordered up to a maximum charge of £3.00.
OVERSEAS & EIRE – £2.00 for the first book, £1.00 for the second book, and 50p for each additional book.

Name...

Address...

....

....

If you would prefer to pay by credit card, please complete:
Please debit my Visa/Access/Diner's Card/American Express (delete as applicable) card no:

Signature..

Expiry Date...